# Strange Deception

# STRANGE DECEPTION

**Alicia Engelhardt**

ROM
F
ENG

***AVALON BOOKS***
THOMAS BOUREGY AND COMPANY, INC.
401 LAFAYETTE STREET
NEW YORK, NEW YORK 10003

JY

PRINTED IN THE UNITED STATES OF AMERICA
BY HADDON CRAFTSMEN, SCRANTON, PENNSYLVANIA

# Strange Deception

# CHAPTER ONE

A ghostly cloud swirled across the full, luminous moon, blocking it momentarily, turning the warm June night a rich, velvety black. Pounding rock music mixed with boisterous laughter vibrated the stairs of the old weathered porch where Kelcy Kendal sat alone gazing up, her back against the wooden paint-chipped railing. She held in one hand a glass of ice water, occasionally sipping the refreshing liquid to get some relief from the humid air.

It could have been a night in the tropics with gentle sea breezes and soft moonlight, she thought dreamily. But, alas, it wasn't. It was just an ordinary Friday night in Porton, Wisconsin, and inside the large two-story white house, a dreadful party was in full swing.

Just minutes ago, Kelcy had quietly escaped the

overcrowded, smoke-filled rooms and the depress-ingly phony people mingling about, with potent drinks and forced laughter, trying to convince themselves they were having a great time.

"I really didn't want to come, so why did I?" Kelcy whispered her question to the moon as it reappeared to cast its silvery glow over the dewy lawn.

But she need not have asked, for she knew why. She was desperate to find a job, having lost her previous one through unusual circumstances, and her friend Sandra Frye had insisted that this party would solve all her job-hunting problems.

Sandra's enthusiasm had been infectious earlier that evening when she had issued the last-minute, secondhand invitation along with the promise that one of the guests—a friend of a friend—a man who happened to work at a temporary-job place-ment service, would be attending. He had lots of contacts, Sandra had assured Kelcy. And if by chance he didn't show, she'd added, there might be other people who would know of a job opening for a skilled secretary.

Some solution to all her job-hunting problems, Kelcy thought now. Why, she hadn't even seen Sandra since they had arrived together over an hour ago! And as far as job contacts went, not a soul who had shouted to Kelcy above the deafening music looked as if he or she could hold down a job let alone tell her of one that was available.

Suddenly she felt a strong urge to laugh at the strange, cruel twists of fate. Until two weeks ago, Kelcy's life had been wonderfully simple and secure. She had worked as a private secretary to kindly James Miles, a soft-spoken, good-natured little man in his early fifties, and she'd had no financial worries. But James Miles had turned out to be a thief.

Even now, looking back, Kelcy still found it hard to believe her former boss was a crafty embezzler of the cleverest type. But his sudden disappearance, the missing company funds, his farewell note— they had all pointed to the shocking truth, leaving no cause for doubt.

Straitlaced Mr. Miles! A chill ran through Kelcy as she thought of him sitting nonchalantly at his desk day after day. How he had fooled everyone! He had ruined a rising company and put many good people out of work, including herself. Had he even cared that she had been drilled for hours by police detectives and was suspected of being his accomplice?

How idiotic their insinuations were, she thought in retrospect. Had she been his accomplice, she would be with Miles now in South America, where rumor had placed him, gazing up at a real tropical moon—not at this wretched party.

Above the sounds of the music, a screen door suddenly slammed. Kelcy turned to see a tall, slendar young man in a well-cut suit move toward the stairs. He looked faintly familiar and very much out of place. She recognized him then to be the man she had noticed earlier, making the rounds inside with a slinky blonde hanging tightly to his arm. Somehow he had shaken himself free of the girl and was now alone. He stopped before descending the stairs and smiled down at Kelcy.

"Hi!" he said. "So here's where all the angels are hiding." He walked down a few steps and sat down near her. "And why are you out here all alone? Waiting for someone . . . perhaps?"

"No," Kelcy said. "I was just thinking about leaving."

"Now, what a coincidence." He smiled crookedly, his rakish face both enigmatic and charming. "As a matter of fact, I was just about to leave myself."

He was an attractive man with blue eyes, curly hair, a bold smile, and a firm chin, and Kelcy could not help wondering how many women he had under his spell. And although she guessed him to be only twenty-four or twenty-five, two or three years older than she, her intuition said he was far more experienced than his boyish face suggested.

"Well, I'm not stopping you from leaving," she said.

Reaching in his pocket, he took out a slim cigar, balanced it between gleaming teeth, and produced a fancy gold lighter. An amber-blue flame instantly came to life at his touch. "I had a feeling this wasn't your type of party."

"And what do you mean by that?" Kelcy responded stiffly, feeling he was making insincere small talk.

He blew a puff of gray smoke into the night air. "Well, when a girl sits alone on the stairs, ignoring a sea of people inside, it's not hard to see she's having a rotten time. Satisfy my curiosity. Why did a classy girl like you come to this boring party?"

Kelcy looked away. It was uncanny the way he had read her thoughts. But she was not about to let him know that.

"I really don't know what you mean," she replied, taking a long sip of water. "I was mingling earlier. Not to the extent you were, but—"

"Oh, were you?" he broke in. "You could have fooled me. I was watching you for a while inside."

Kelcy shrugged. "You're right. I confess. I shouldn't have come." She glared at him. "Is that more to your liking?"

He said nothing, but Kelcy felt the need to go on.

"I don't know anyone in there. And I'm not sure I'd want to—except for Sandra. She's the real reason I came in the first place. I'm looking for work, and she was so sure I could make some contacts tonight. She said she knew some guy who works for a temporary-job employment agency. But no one like that seems to be here."

"I see," he said, studying her long chestnut hair, her dusky-green eyes, her soft-curved lips, and every flawless feature in her oval face. "And what kind of work do you do?"

"Well, I used to work at Royal Art Supplies until it folded two weeks ago. I was James Miles's private secretary. You might have read about the vice president who embezzled the company funds and is thought to be somewhere in South America. It was in the newspaper. Well, that was him. So now I'm out of a job. My friend Sandra convinced me to come to this party to meet someone who might have some job leads. But that hasn't worked out."

The young man dropped his smoldering cigar to the ground and extinguished it with his shoe. Then he said, "You know, I think I can help you with that job. Let me drive you home and we'll talk."

"Really?" Kelcy's eyes brightened. "I mean, you wouldn't happen to be the guy that works for the job-placement service Sandra said would be here tonight?"

"No, hardly that," he said, suppressing a smile.

She looked pretty and perplexed wondering if she should accept his offer to drive her home. Finally, she said, "I'd have to tell Sandra I'm leaving. She'll worry if I just disappear."

"She won't even miss you. Let's go."

Feeling uneasy, Kelcy looked back at the house as she was led over to the sidewalk. It didn't seem proper to go off without telling Sandra, but perhaps the man was right. After all, Sandra had been quick to desert her after they had arrived.

"Don't look so worried, honey," the man coaxed. "No one will even miss you."

As they walked down the poorly lit street into the dewy night, a thought struck Kelcy like a thunderbolt. "What about your blond girlfriend? Won't she be angry?"

"Forget her," he snapped. "I already have."

His callous remark made Kelcy flinch. Such hardness!

As they continued walking toward the car, the stern old voice of Kelcy's Great-Aunt Bess came back to haunt her. "Don't ever take rides from strangers, girl!"

Well, even Bess didn't know everything, Kelcy reflected moodily, angry with herself for having remembered at all. But it was hard to forget the years after the death of her parents in a plane crash. When the accident happened, she was just fifteen and went to board with her great-aunt. She and Bess tolerated one another, for Kelcy had always been a quiet, obedient teen. However, no real affection had existed between them. Kelcy knew the old woman had offered her a home through a sense of duty only.

Those first two years at Bess's had dragged on uneventfully. It was not until Kelcy had completed high school at seventeen that she showed any signs of rebellion. Full of youthful ambition, she knew she could never be content continuing with the factory job Bess had secured for her through an acquaintance. And that September she had announced her plans for enrollment in Wilton College where she would study art—if only Bess would lend her the money.

Bess wanted Kelcy to keep her factory job. She said she had no money available to be thrown away on college tuition.

Argument upon argument followed, and Bess would not be budged. But neither would Kelcy. After careful thought and many trips to the student-counseling office on campus, she decided she could do it on her own.

Immediately she moved from Bess's house into the home of a professor and his family where she did some housekeeping and baby-sitting in exchange for room and board, along with a small salary. It was a start, the first step toward her goal.

From the day Kelcy had chosen to make her own way in the world, her life had been an endless struggle of part-time jobs, full-day classes, and various business courses at night. There had been no time for friends, parties, or the other things girls of her age enjoyed.

At the end of four hard years, with the aid of scholarships and student loans, she received, with honors, her prized art degree.

Because of the few job opportunities and tough competition in her field, especially for beginners, as Kelcy had expected, she was thankful she had studied typing and shorthand and bookkeeping. When a secretarial position opened at Royal Art Supplies, she was happy to take it.

James Miles had agreed to hire her for three months on a trial basis. Then her job became permanent, and the next nine months had been pleasant and rewarding, with Kelcy doing her artwork at night and on the weekends. But now, of course, she no longer had a job.

Kelcy became aware that she and the young man had reached a car. He was fumbling for the keys in his pocket. Casually her glance flicked to the vehicle. It was a metallic gray, its design quite elegant.

"Beautiful car!" Admiration softened her green eyes.

In a cool voice, the man replied, "Yes, isn't it?" He opened the door and helped her in. It had the distinct smell of newness.

Kelcy had never seen an interior so exquisite. Its dark leather upholstery, rich wood panels, and plush rug made her feel as if she had stepped into a dream. She settled back in the comfortable seat and waited as her companion slipped in beside her and took the wheel.

"Expensive, I'll bet," Kelcy said.

He wasn't really listening as he fumbled on the dashboard for the light switch. "Uh, what, honey?"

"Expensive car, I said."

"Oh, yeah, I'm sure it is."

She smiled, contented, not trying to pry or be overly inquisitive, but unable to help herself. "What type of car is this?"

"Huh—what did you say?" the man replied absently as he eased the car from its parking place and headed down the street, seeming a bit unsure of himself.

"Oh, nothing," she said quietly, not wishing to break his concentration, for apparently he was not used to driving his new car yet.

He relaxed a little and fleetingly smiled at her. "Give me a direction, honey."

"Oh, I'm sorry," Kelcy said. "Just keep going straight. I live in the old section of town on Elm. We're on the right course."

They had driven several blocks when her companion suddenly spun his head around and muttered a harsh oath. With the quickness of a panther, he turned his gaze back to the road ahead, stepping down hard on the gas pedal. The car jerked forward, increasing in speed.

Confused and frightened, Kelcy looked back.

Red lights flashed ominously in the distance. Then came the sound of a siren. A police car was behind them.

She stared at the man beside her. "What's going on? Is that car following you?"

"Yep, they must have seen the plates," he admitted. "I was afraid that might happen when I saw them cruising back there, and I'm in no mood to get stopped. Look, honey, fasten your seat belt. I think I can outrun them."

# CHAPTER TWO

At first Kelcy thought her companion might be joking about outrunning the police. But when he turned sharply onto a side street, she knew that he was not. Given little choice, Kelcy fastened her seat belt with trembling fingers.

Reaching dangerous speeds, the chase continued through one dark alley after another. Suddenly, a man walking his dog came into sight. The driver twisted the steering wheel, causing the car to swerve wildly, before he slammed on his brakes to avoid striking them. Tires squealed, the man yelled, and Kelcy gasped. She had had enough! The driver had to be stopped. The siren was close behind.

"What's the matter?" she shrieked. "Hey, don't you know you're making things worse by running

11

like this? They might only have wanted to tell you a taillight's out or something."

"No chance, honey," the man shouted, then made another sharp turn. "As far as they're concerned, the car is hot!"

"What?" Kelcy snapped. "You mean you stole this car?" Panic struck. Her heart beat furiously as they raced out of the city, the red lights and siren right behind them.

"Blast those guys, but they're good!" the driver shouted, almost with admiration, as they wildly streaked down the highway.

Kelcy glanced in terror at the speedometer. It was wavering well over one hundred.

"Please stop!" she screamed. "They won't give up, and you're going to kill us all!"

"Be quiet!" he snorted rudely as the car spurted forward effortlessly. "I know this road, and it'll be okay. There's a turnoff up ahead. We'll shake them there for sure!"

He was enjoying this, Kelcy realized. She never should have gone with him. Bess had been right about not riding with strangers! Well, he had to stop soon. No one could keep up this pace forever, she told herself.

Just then her wishes, like magic, turned true. Without warning, he slammed on the brakes. Then the sickening sound of grinding metal burst upon the darkness as the car slid down a long ravine, rolled over, and stopped at the bottom in the midst of some underbrush.

Struck by a blunt object, Kelcy screamed. Slowly everything began to whirl around her and grow dimmer. In the tunnel of darkness she soon lost all feeling, all consciousness.

When Kelcy awoke, she was lying on a starchy antiseptic-smelling sheet. A dull pain throbbed inside her head, and all around her there was white. For a minute or so she had difficulty focusing her eyes.

"She's coming around," a low voice muttered.

"Good—then we can get some answers!" a second voice rasped.

Horrid memories of a car accident swept through Kelcy like a giant wave. Had she dreamt all that, or had it truly happened? The memories became clearer. It had happened, all right. The images of flashing lights were still with her.

Kelcy made an effort to sit up, but she fell back against the abrasive sheet, too weak for such a maneuver.

A man dressed in white, middle-aged, wearing glasses and a thick red beard, took her hand carefully, eased it up, then slipped out a needle that had been inserted in a vein near her wrist.

He said, "Well, young lady, we won't be needing this IV anymore. I'm Dr. Bell, and you've had a nasty bump on your head. Try to be quiet. The tests we ran show everything's okay. You've had a mild concussion, but there's been no actual damage to your brain. You're a very lucky girl, considering what could have happened."

From out of the corner, another man materialized. He was short and stocky, with iron-gray hair.

He came closer to the bed, his face unsmiling and strained.

"In case you don't know this, young woman, you're in big trouble. So I would advise you to tell us the whole truth. Is this your purse?"

He held up the small, thin leather clutch bag Kelcy had taken to the party.

"Yes," she said tremulously. "It's mine."

"And your name . . ."

She swallowed hard. "Kelcy Kendal." She tried to move, only to discover her body ached mercilessly all over. Even speaking was an effort, but she slowly went on. "Where am I? Is this a hospital?"

The short gray-haired man was writing things down on a pad. "I'm asking the questions here. Well, the name checks out with the license in the wallet. Now who was your accomplice in this auto theft?"

Kelcy blinked, her eyes large and anxious. She felt the color flood her face. There was that word again—accomplice. She had heard it tossed about two weeks ago in connection with the embezzlement at Royal Art Supplies. Now someone else was accusing her of being an accomplice.

"I don't know," she said, aware of how feeble that sounded even to her own ears. "But you can't think that I played any part in stealing that car! You can't possibly—"

His stubby hand waved slowly back and forth to silence her. "You don't know!" He mocked her words threateningly. "But you know that the car was stolen. You mean to say that you won't tell us anything else."

The cottony dryness of Kelcy's mouth forced her to swallow again. "I don't know," she repeated. "The guy never told me who he was. We met at a party and he offered me a ride home."

From somewhere in the shadows behind a screen, Kelcy heard movement and a muttered oath. The voice was pitched low and had a disturbing smooth silkiness to it.

"You're not going to get anywhere with her," the deep voice went on.

The stocky man hovering by Kelcy's bedside turned around. "Hawk, as your lawyer, I'll see to it that she does talk. Believe me, they won't get away with this. Justice will be done."

Kelcy was about to cry. She hadn't stolen anyone's car. Couldn't they see that she was no thief? The most she had been guilty of was being a bad judge of character. She certainly seemed to be trusting the wrong men of late.

"Will you please listen to me? I didn't steal anything," she whispered fervently.

"Oh, come off it!" the lawyer snarled, glaring at her with hard black eyes. "You were found strapped into the evidence. Your boyfriend may have gotten away, but you didn't. And the police will get him, too!"

"Gentlemen, please," Dr. Bell broke in. "This young woman is recovering from shock. Can't this wait?" He picked up his chart from the bedside table and moved toward the door. "I realize your problem here. However, I can allow you just five minutes longer with this patient. She needs rest. Come back in the morning. Now, if you'll excuse me, this seems to be the night for emergencies." He walked from the room, closing the door behind him.

Kelcy couldn't have felt more deserted, like a slice of meat tossed to hungry wolves, and she was very much afraid.

"You say you don't know your friend's name," the lawyer scoffed. "Can you describe him to us?"

Kelcy frowned, sinking down into the hard pillow as deeply as she could. She chose her words with care. "He was average, I guess. Wavy hair, a bit too long. Nice-looking. That's all I can remember. We just met—"

"Color of hair?"

"Brown, I think, or it could have been sandy." She moved her hand restlessly as she tried to recall. "It was dark out on the porch, and I—"

"Do you actually think you can believe anything she says?" The mysterious owner of the deep voice stepped out of the shadows to the foot of the bed. "She's just described three-fourths of the male population of this county."

But not you, Kelcy thought to herself, for she could see nothing average about him.

Tall and commanding, standing there in the bright light with that sarcastic smile on his dark, handsome face, his gray eyes gleaming, he was struggling hard to keep a firm control over his temper.

His hands looked big and strong, and she eyed them warily, sensing uneasily that, given the slightest provocation, he would joyfully strangle her. But in all fairness, she conceded, he had the right to be angry at someone—but that someone was not in this room.

Kelcy asked him softly: "Was that your car that —that creep stole?"

He did not answer. Kelcy lay helpless, miserable under his punishing gaze. She wanted so much to turn her head to the pillow and weep, but her pride would not allow that. Never could she let him see her break into tears—tears caused by him.

"You're darn right it was his car!" the stocky lawyer told her. "Do you have any idea who this man is, young woman?"

Kelcy shook her head slowly, thinking it was a very dumb question. Of course, she did not know this young man. She had never set eyes on him before tonight. Yet it puzzled her that there was something oddly familiar about his features—the thick dark hair, the firm-set mouth, the straight nose, and the forceful chin. He did remind her of someone whom just now she could not remember.

The lawyer continued talking, something he seemed to enjoy. "Let me present Mr. Charles Hawken Westbrook, one of the leading industrialists in this state. To his friends and business associates, he's simply known as Hawk. He heads Westbrook Industries. Have you, by chance, ever heard of his company, young woman?"

Ignoring the heavy sarcasm in his voice, Kelcy said, "I think I have. I think that—" She stopped speaking abruptly.

She was about to say that she had filed a job application with the personnel department of that company over a week ago. The man who had interviewed her had beady little eyes and a nasty smirk, she recalled. His attitude became very negative when he discovered her former boss was the embezzler James Miles.

"Go on," the lawyer prompted now. "You were saying . . ."

"They manufacture heavy machinery. Is that the company you mean?"

His brows shot up. "Among other things. Well, I see you do know." The stocky man sounded surprised. "So know this, too. You're in serious trouble. That Mercedes, only a week out of the dealer's showroom, was worth more than you've ever seen. And it will cost plenty to fix!" He paused for emphasis. "As yet we haven't pressed charges. We've been holding off. But as soon as Hawk decides to prosecute, a snap of the fingers will bring the police in here to arrest you. Criminal law is a bit out of my line, but I imagine the charge will be grand theft or party to the theft, something on that order, girl. Think about it!"

Kelcy felt cold. She shivered as her green eyes leapt from one man to the other. She was thinking about it—thinking of nothing else! What could she possibly say to them? Already they had pronounced her guilty, tried and convicted her on circumstantial evidence. Pretty strong evidence, though.

Suddenly she felt more frightened than she had ever been in her entire life. She tried as hard as she could to meet Hawk Westbrook's hostile gaze, but tears came instead.

"I'm so sorry about your car, Mr. Westbrook," she managed to say. "I begged him to stop. I can't tell you anything else because I just don't know any more."

Hawk Westbrook was about to say something when the door was opened by Dr. Bell. "Gentlemen, time is up!"

"Okay, Doc," the lawyer called, "we're about through." He turned to put his pad and some papers in a small briefcase. "What do you want to do about this, Hawk? Call in the police? It's up to you. But that's what I'd advise."

"Let it go for tonight," Hawk replied, his voice thick with contempt. "I'll decide what I want done in the morning. It's a bet she won't be going anywhere."

"Should I have an officer posted outside just in case she might try—"

"No, there's no need for that," Hawk said.

And the two men walked out the door.

Dr. Bell entered after exchanging words with them in the corridor. "Try to get some rest." He sounded totally objective. "The way things look, you'll be needing it for the session ahead of you." He, too, then turned on his heel, switched off the glaring light, and strode through the door, closing it tightly behind him.

Kelcy lay still in the dark room, listening to the erratic beating of her heart. Again the tears came. And a terrified cold sweat.

Horrid thoughts tumbled around inside her head. Kelcy wished she had never set eyes on that man at the party. If he'd had to steal a car, why couldn't it have been a worthless old rattletrap, not a brand new Mercedes belonging to the formidable Charles

Hawken Westbrook? What was it his ruthless lawyer had said? She would be arrested and charged with grand theft! That thought did not bear thinking about, it was so horrible—so very horrible. Powerful, wealthy men like Westbrook would stop at nothing, including victimizing the innocent, to get revenge.

Hawk Westbrook's hauntingly handsome face suddenly loomed up before Kelcy, magnified and threatening. Even if she could prove somehow that she had not known the car was stolen when accepting the ride, would he ever let it be over? No, she doubted it. There would be questions—endless questions—demands for a better description of the real thief, things she could not tell them.

She shivered as a chill moved up her spine. Deep down, Kelcy knew the worst was yet to come.

## CHAPTER THREE

It seemed an incredibly long night to Kelcy. At one point a thin-faced nurse ventured in, offering water and a sedative. Obediently, she swallowed the tasteless pill, but she did not get very much sleep.

On Saturday she opened her eyes feeling lost and miserable. The shade was drawn in the small room, and sunlight peeped softly around its edges. From force of habit, Kelcy wondered if the temperature outside was pleasantly warm. Then she gloomily reminded herself that it really didn't matter, anyway, for she might never see daylight again—at least, if Hawk Westbrook had his way.

One nurse helped her wash and another checked her vital signs. But Kelcy was too groggy to ask them any questions.

Sometime later a stout woman dressed in blue entered her room carrying a food tray.

The woman smiled cheerfully. "Are you ready to eat?"

Kelcy nodded yes, then asked, "How long must I stay here?"

"Anxious to leave us?" the woman said.

Kelcy thought to herself, Lady, you don't know how anxious. But out loud she merely replied, "Yes, I'd like to go home."

"Only the doctor can tell you when. But let me see if he has any notation on your chart." She busied herself by arranging the tray for Kelcy. Then she read Kelcy's chart. "This doesn't say much, but I'd guess he could release you tomorrow since you're listed as an emergency admittance for twenty-four-hour observation—oh, I almost forgot! There's a gentleman outside waiting to see you. But—"

"There is?" Kelcy broke in, surprised at the news until she realized that Westbrook and his attorney were probably back. Her cheeks paled. "He wouldn't happen to be tall and—"

"Handsome," the nursing assistant finished. "Yes, he's all of that and more. You could put on some lipstick if you'd feel more comfortable. Your makeup should be in the closet. But the visitors aren't allowed in till a bit later."

With the assistance of the kind woman, Kelcy put on a dab of makeup and combed her hair. She was picking at her plate of cold eggs when there was a knock on the door. Her heart began to pound. She expected Charles Hawken Westbrook and his lawyer to come rushing in with a dozen policemen. But when the door did open, Kelcy could not believe her eyes. Was it an hallucination? Or had the car thief really come to visit her?

"You!" she cried.

"Be quiet, please!" the young man said, glancing over his shoulder in a nervous manner. Then he closed the door behind him and came over to her side. "We've got to talk and fast!"

Kelcy stared at him incredulously. "You must be mad coming here! Everyone in the county is out searching for you."

"I doubt that." He smiled crookedly. "Now just listen . . . Kelcy, is it?"

"Yes, but how did you find out my name?"

"I called here last night twice to see how you were. First, I said I was a cop checking up on an accident report, and I sort of manipulated the receptionist into giving me information. Then later, I said I was your brother."

He would do that, she thought angrily. "That was real smart. I don't even have a brother!"

"It doesn't matter," he laughed.

"Well, I can certainly give them an accurate description of you now," she snarled, studying him closely, noting the red T-shirt and corded jeans and the fact that he had gotten a haircut. "Do you know whose car you stole?"

"Of course, I do," he said. "But I didn't steal it, not really. I just borrowed it without telling anyone."

"Well, I'm going to tell everyone!" She grabbed for the service bell.

He reached over quickly, clamped his hand on

hers, and stopped her from pressing the button. "Kelcy, honey, hear what I have to say first."

"It doesn't really matter what you do." She pushed his hand away. "They'll be here at any moment and they'll see you."

"I know, so quit wasting time! What did you tell them?"

She said, "Just what do you think I told them? And don't ever call me 'honey' again!"

He shrugged. "It sure couldn't have been much, I gather, from what my old man said. Hawk was furious last night, madder than Dad had ever seen him. Mainly because he couldn't get any straight answers from you. You did all right, Kelcy."

Kelcy looked at him, her green eyes unable to hide their surprise. "You . . . you know Hawk?"

"Of course, I know him," he said ruefully. "Hawk's my cousin. Didn't you notice the family resemblance? I'm Glen Westbrook, by the way."

Kelcy's head started to throb. "How could you steal from your own cousin?" she demanded angrily.

Glen sat down in the chair at the side of the bed. Not even the slightest suggestion of guilt touched his face. "He was supposed to be in San Francisco on business. I know this is difficult for you to understand, and I don't have time to fill you in, but I'm going to ask you to do me one big favor, Kelcy."

"Why should I do anything for you?" Kelcy snarled. "You ran off and left me for dead last night, and you didn't even have the decency to explain things."

"I didn't leave you for dead!" Glen protested. "I checked to see if you were breathing, and I did call here to make sure my diagnosis was right. And about the other thing, I have my reasons for not wanting to be placed in this area last night."

There was a pause while he looked at her thoughtfully, gently taking her hand. "Kelcy, I have no right to ask you this, but I'm going to anyway. Don't tell them you were with me last night, please. I'll make it worth your while."

A warm rush of color flooded her cheeks. What kind of a person did Glen think she was? Did he really believe he could buy her silence? And with Westbrook money at that! Such arrogance—bred strong and true into the family line, to be sure.

"Promise me you won't tell," he urged softly.

She frowned and tried to free her hand, but he wouldn't let her go. "No! I won't promise anything. They're talking about sending me to jail."

"Hey, come on," Glen said. "Take that worried look off your pretty face. Hawk's a hard-nosed businessman, ruthless when he wants to be, but he's not made entirely out of ice. Just flash those lynx eyes at him the way you're doing now, and you won't have any problems!"

"No!" Kelcy snapped. "I can't. You don't have any idea how he and his lawyer threatened me."

"Oh, I think I do!" He seemed serious now. "But trust me. I won't let them do anything. If things get out of hand, I'll admit what I did. You can't lose on a deal like that."

Kelcy knew she could lose plenty. It was a stupid and big mistake to consider his outrageous proposition and yet her curiosity betrayed her. Could she trust Glen enough to do as he asked? Certainly it couldn't hurt to hear him out.

"What do you want from me?" she asked.

A ray of hope flashed in his eyes. "Just say as little as possible. Don't tell them any more than you already have. And in three weeks or so, I'll be able to tell Hawk what really happened. Just imagine him having to apologize to you then. Wouldn't you like that, Kelcy? Turn the cards on him for a change. Will you let me handle all the details?"

She didn't know why she was considering Glen's request. She needn't have. And from her point of view, it would be much better if she didn't. But something about Glen had touched her, possibly his anxiety—or was it the thought of the arrogant Charles Hawken Westbrook having to humble himself by apologizing to her for all the unfair accusations he had made and the cruel things his lawyer had said?

A wicked smile touched her lips. She gazed at Glen wryly. "If I do agree to protect you—and I haven't yet—but if I do, you promise you'll tell your cousin the whole truth, clearing me?"

"Of course, I'll promise," he said. "But I need time, at least three weeks. I'll explain why later."

There was no time for Kelcy to reply, for at that moment the door swung open and Hawk Westbrook, followed by his stocky lawyer, came striding in. He stopped short. An unfathomable shadow passed over his hard face as his eyes fell upon his cousin.

"What the devil's going on here, Glen?" he demanded sharply.

With a delicious terror mounting inside her, Kelcy wondered how Glen was going to get out of this one and watched in awe as he rose to his feet, calmly extending his hand.

"Good to see you, Hawk," Glen said. "I was looking for you, and your office said you'd be here."

Hawk relaxed and shook his cousin's hand. "Couldn't it wait?"

"I suppose it could have. But, frankly, when I got home this morning and Dad told me what happened, my curiosity piqued."

For the first time since he had entered the room, Hawk Westbrook glanced toward Kelcy. His mouth tightened in a hard line, his icy gray eyes as cold as steel. Then he turned back to his cousin. "I guess I should ask how your exams went," Hawk said.

Glen said, "Fine, fine. Finished up the final one last night at about nine. I caught the morning flight home, and now that my family obligations are over, I can start plans for the future. Actually that's what I was coming to see you about."

"Right." Hawk seemed quite pleased.

By now Kelcy had begun to piece bits together. Glen's request that she cover for him apparently stemmed from a family matter. Although she knew little else, she did know that Glen was taking no exam at nine last night—he was at the party in the company of a slinky blonde.

"So," Glen said conversationally, "your car was

stolen. By the way, I thought you were in San Francisco."

"I was," Hawk crisply answered, "but I concluded my business early. There didn't seem much point in dragging it out."

Glen was smiling for reasons known only to himself. "No, suppose not. I was just interrogating your little suspect here. I'm convinced that she's totally innocent."

Clearing his throat in the background, the lawyer opened his black briefcase. "Glen, this is none of your affair."

"Oh, Bill, now let's not be so darned inflexible. The poor kid is as white as a sheet and trembling." He turned to Hawk. "She isn't a hardened criminal. Show some mercy!"

"And if it were one of your sports cars she and her pal stole and damaged, I suppose you'd be standing there showing all that mercy, right, Glen?" Hawk countered.

Glen raked a hand through his brown hair. "I suspect I would. And, hell, I saw that car in the driveway. There wasn't that much damage. Maybe a dent or two."

"Four thousand dollars' worth!" the lawyer shot out. "The appraisers just finished with it. Who do you expect to pay for this, Glen?"

He shrugged. "Hawk's insurance. He pays high enough premiums."

"Even so," the lawyer growled, "There's a deductible clause that makes us responsible for half."

Glen turned toward Kelcy with an apologetic

smile. "Do you have the money to cover this, Miss Kendal?"

Frightened, she shook her head negatively. She felt trapped, wanting to say something, yet not knowing what. Her pleading eyes gazed at Glen.

"You know, I had nothing to do with this," she said.

"Hush," he said gently. "Lie back and relax. Don't get overexcited."

Hawl walked over to the bedside and stopped, one hand resting on the pocket of his elegant suit, a perfect match to the gray eyes mocking Kelcy. "I don't appreciate your interference, Glen. And just what is your interest in this girl, anyway?"

Glen looked affronted. "Interest? Me? You misjudge things, Hawk. My only interest is in justice."

"Since when?"

"We're wasting time here," the stocky lawyer snorted. "Call in the police and have done with it."

Glen turned on him angrily. "Sure, do that! Throw her behind bars. Now that makes a lot of sense! You heard her say she didn't have any money, so she sits there waiting for a trial because she can't make bail. Now that's really going to get your damages paid for." He looked grimly at his cousin. "And, Hawk, is that the kind of publicity you want for the family?"

Hawk gave Kelcy a sharp look. "No, as a matter of fact. That's exactly what I don't want. Give me an alternative, Miss Kendal, and I shall consider it. Are you sure you don't have more information about the accident?"

Kelcy glanced at Glen nervously. He hadn't done

too much to champion her cause thus far. The temptation to tell the truth grew strong, but he looked so much like a vulnerable little boy.

"I'm sorry, Mr. Westbrook," she answered in a whisper. "There's nothing I can add to what I told you last night."

Hawk impatiently crossed to the window and gazed out. He was furious but controlling his anger well. "If that's the way you want it, Miss Kendal." He shrugged and spun around. "Bill, handle it any way you like." Then he started for the door.

"Hawk, come on," Glen said. "Give her a chance!"

"I gave her a chance—too many chances!"

"Yes, but did she explain why she went to that party before she met that . . . guy?" Glen persisted. "Did you even ask her?"

"What the blazes do I care why she went!" Hawk exploded.

"Kelcy." Glen turned to her. He frowned as he noted the mistiness of her eyes. He didn't want her breaking down on him now after all his careful planning. "Tell him why you went."

She didn't want to answer. She had done nothing to deserve all this trouble. It wasn't fair! A tear slowly crept down her cheek.

Hawk came to stand before her, his face hard and unyielding. "I'm not waiting much longer!" he rapped out impatiently.

Kelcy's throat ached. She swallowed. "I—I went to that party to find a job. I'd lost my old job because of the embezzlement. When I met this man, he said we'd talk about it on the way home."

"Oh, no! Do I have to hear this, too!" Hawk growled.

"Wait, Hawk!" Glen said. "It's not as bad as it sounds. She just said it wrong. Kelcy, straighten him out."

But she had no intention of straightening him out. Let him think what he liked. Let his lawyer call the police!

No! She didn't want that either, she realized. She was under enough suspicion because of the Miles case.

In a panic, without even stopping for breath, Kelcy quickly ran through the facts regarding her previous job. Then she explained that she'd gone to the party in the hopes of meeting a man who worked for an employment agency.

When she had finished, Hawk looked at her, scowling. "So you were James Miles's former secretary."

Kelcy inhaled sharply. Why had he said it like that? Hawk's face was inscrutable as he watched her. His daring eyes roved over her insolently.

"And you were in my office the other day looking for work," he stated bluntly.

Kelcy stared at him in stunned silence. How did he know that? She had only talked to one man in personnel, and that interview had been a hopeless one.

"You really baffle me," Hawk said. Conflicting emotions played across his face. "Why would a girl like you, with an art degree, be working as a secretary? Unless there were terrific side benefits?"

The whole room suddenly grew quiet, all eyes fixed upon Kelcy.

"I had nothing to do with embezzling any funds, if that's what you're thinking," she said stiffly.

And that was her last denial of guilt, Kelcy vowed stubbornly. She wasn't going to tell Hawk anything more. She had taken that job out of necessity. There were school loans to pay back and living expenses, and the position paid well. Meanwhile, she'd done some painting in her free time. Maybe one day she'd be able to make money from her artwork. But that was in the future. That was her dream. Only, these men wouldn't understand dreams. They were businessmen—all hard, cold fact.

"What else do you think you know about me?" Kelcy asked, not looking at Hawk, her voice unsteady.

He scowled thoughtfully. "If I recall correctly, you live alone in a low-rent section of town. You worked your way through college at various jobs— office, waitressing, etc. You graduated last year with honors, having majored in art. You also have impressive typing and stenographic skills, and you're twenty-two, which seems to me a very young age to be taking up a life of crime."

She cringed, feeling the sting of his words, hating him.

"No, I don't keep a personal dossier on everyone who steps into my office building, if that's what you think, Miss Kendal. But I read the application you submitted to Hatton in personnel. I believe he said as he handed it to me that I should read it for a good laugh. I wasn't too interested, just curious like anyone would be when a business scandal breaks. Now I'm beginning to wish Hatton had found a spot for you. I might have saved myself some costly car repairs!"

The cold whiteness of the room seemed to close in around her. Kelcy felt angry and humiliated. He was making fun of her!

Suddenly, Glen burst into laughter. "My, what a small world! Poor Kelcy. I could have told you not to waste your time seeking a job with Westbrook Industries—not in Hawk's office, anyway. To work there you'd have to fit the Charles Hawken stereotype of the perfect secretary—quiet, mousy, over forty, and preferably married. The more unattractive, the better. All that and a detestable personality to match. In short, everything you're not, honey!"

"And there's good reason for that," Hawk remarked stiffly. "I've tried all types, always with the same results. The young, single ones can't keep their romances out of the office. Or they get interested in me. Their work suffers. They're of no use to me or the company."

"How insensitive of them!" Glen mocked. "When they see an eligible bachelor, both rich and powerful, the head of his own company, they just can't help swooning at his feet. Imagine the burden on you! What a rough business, eh, Hawk?"

Hawk's eyes glinted bitterly. "Your only business, Glen, is to find new ways to spend your enormous unearned income. Your chief ambition in life is driving race cars too fast."

"Oh, yes, yes," Glen responded, anxious to turn

their discussion into a family squabble. "Let's talk about expensive little whims, shall we? What about that house and old mill you bought three years ago up in Door County? You sank more money into that place, hotshot, than I ever spent in my life."

Glen spun around, his gaze leveled on Kelcy. "If you like art, now that's where you should go. All the dedicated ones—those painters, sculptors, weavers, potters, jewelry makers—find their way up there. The Door Peninsula swarms with the lot during the summer months. And Hawk, imagine him—not an artistic bone in his body—and he buys an old mill and house up there that dates back to the 1800's. He sinks a small fortune into restoring it, and for what? He's been up there maybe a half dozen times in his life. Our poor Aunt Jenna spends her summers there, isolated from everyone, just to give him an excuse. Oh, well, what's the use of talking about it?"

"I always wanted to spend my summers there," Hawk said. "But the business—"

"Damn the business!" Glen shouted. "It always comes first with you. You are your father's son right to the core! Too bad my father doesn't have a son like that, too, isn't it, Hawk? But just tell me what all that fanatic dedication got your dad. No, let me tell you—millions, yes, that he could have easily done without, loneliness, and an early grave. Just watch that it doesn't happen to you, cousin. You're headed for it!"

A deafening silence fell over the room. Then, as if on cue, the lawyer spoke up:

"I think it's time I phoned the police detectives.

This girl is the cause of enough trouble." He reached for the phone.

Glen swiftly caught his hand, stopping him. Then he turned to his cousin. "Look, Hawk, let's be reasonable. Okay, okay, I lost my temper. We both had a turn at it. But now if we can toss the swords down, will you listen to me?"

Almost reluctantly, Hawk sighed, "If you've got something more to say, then say it!"

Finally, Kelcy thought, Glen was going to tell the truth. A sense of relief flowed through her.

"All right, Hawk," Glen began, "you keep saying you want to spend some time up at your country house and old mill. Then do it! Go up there and blow the dust off the shelves. Play with your horses or whatever pleases you. Enjoy it! Aunt Jenna would be thrilled with the company."

Hawk sighed heavily. "And what about my responsibilities here? I suppose you think I should follow your example and just drop everything to do whatever I please. Why, I can't even go to San Francisco for a few days without coming back to find my car stolen!"

Kelcy got the full impact of his accusing glance just then and shivered.

"I'm coming to that!" Glen said. "You had the mill office renovated, so why not work from there? What's to prevent you from putting in a direct line, tying right into the computers down here and making the mill your summer headquarters? And—take Kelcy with you as your secretary."

Kelcy's eyes widened. The idea was ludicrous! She work for Hawk Westbrook? Nothing in the world, not even Glen's taunts, could convince him to agree to such a thing. And she would never agree either!

"Glen, don't be ridiculous!" said the stocky lawyer. "Hawk doesn't want to interrupt his schedule, nor would he want a girl like that working for him. It would get monotonous counting the silverware each night."

"I hope that was a joke, Bill," Glen said. "And why not let her work for you, Hawk? How else is she going to pay you for the damage to your Mercedes? Look at it this way. She's made to order. For one thing, she has no choice. For another, you know none of your married secretaries would be willing to give up their happy homes to follow you dutifully up to the woods. Well, maybe they would. But their husbands and kids would protest plenty."

Hawk considered the idea for a moment. "It could be you're making sense for once in your life, Glen. We'll see." His next words were directed at his lawyer. "All right, Bill, draw up a contract and make her sign it. She works for me until the damages are paid." He looked at Kelcy. "And you, Miss Kendal, will either agree to this arrangement on my terms or go to jail. Take your pick!"

But before she had time to reply, Hawk walked through the door, the lawyer in his wake.

Glen turned to Kelcy, smiling triumphantly. "Whew! We did it! I told you I'd get you a job, Kelcy. I had something else in mind, but this is perfect. And don't worry about your salary. You'll get it all back when I'm able to tell him in a few weeks . . ." He stopped in mid-sentence. "You know, for a minute there I thought I'd have to offer to pay that whole repair bill out of my own pocket to get them off your case. Hawk sure would have been suspicious then because that's unlike me. Well, I'd better leave, too, or they'll for sure think something's wrong here."

"There is something wrong!" Kelcy snapped. "It's perfect for you maybe. But not for me. I don't want to work for your cousin!"

"Kelcy," Glen pleaded, "don't be stupid! Trust me. You'll love the Door Peninsula. It's an artist's haven. The scenery is spectacular. What more can I say? And as far as Hawk goes, hey, don't let him get to you!" Glen gently kissed her cheek. "He surprised me, though. I never thought he'd go for my left-field idea, but you never know with that guy. You never know what's in his mind."

Kelcy's eyes grew big with rebellion and fear. She didn't like Hawk. She certainly didn't trust him.

"Kelcy, it'll be all right. Trust me." Glen smiled.

But her doubts only intensified.

# CHAPTER FOUR

Twenty-four hours later Kelcy was released from the hospital. Before that time, the contract had been drawn up, signed, and witnessed.

The day was overcast and rainy, matching her mood. The hospital bill, which seemed enormous for her short stay, had been paid by Hawk Westbrook. Kelcy was very unhappy about that, but her financial state was too precarious for her to insist on repaying him.

When she got home, she took a leisurely bath and a restful nap. Upon awakening, she put on some jeans and an oversized cotton shirt. She was pleased to see it had stopped raining.

Well, it's time to pack, Kelcy told herself. Crossing over to the bedroom closet again, she opened the door and searched for her two blue suitcases. Slowly, reluctantly, she started to pack her

39

summer clothes. Soon she would be leaving these small rooms that she had come to think of as home —for what, she was uncertain.

She had barely finished packing when the phone rang. It was probably Sandra, she thought, calling about the keys to her apartment. Kelcy had phoned Sandra earlier from the hospital to tell her that she was taking a temporary job on the Peninsula. Sandra had suggested she sublet the flat to Lucy, a friend of hers who had had a fight with her fussy roommate. Lucy was looking for a place of her own and would be glad to stay in Kelcy's apartment temporarily. Sandra had said she would phone later after talking to the other girl.

Kelcy walked to the phone and picked up the receiver. "Hello."

"Miss Kendal, it's Hawk Westbrook," he announced boldly in his deep voice. "Is it possible for you to be ready to leave tonight? I know it was arranged that someone would collect you tomorrow morning, but my plans have changed."

Why had he even bothered to ask? It was obvious from his tone that he was giving her no choice! That was the way he did things.

"Yes, it could be possible," she replied stiffly. "When would you be sending someone?"

He hesitated for just a second. "In an hour."

Kelcy's mouth dropped open with surprise. That certainly wasn't much warning! "Well...I..." She was searching for words. "I'll try!"

His tone was crisp and satisfied as he said, "Fine."

He didn't say good-bye or anything else but simply hung up.

Kelcy dashed around, checking through the room, glad that it was a small apartment so that she did not have too many last-minute details to take care of. After a quick visit to Mrs. Berger, the kindly lady across the hall to whom she gave the keys and final instructions in case Sandra should show the apartment to Lucy, Kelcy sat down on the sofa to catch her breath.

The rest was short, for almost immediately a knock shook the door.

"Come in, it's open," Kelcy called, wondering what Mrs. Berger wanted to ask her. She glanced over her shoulder and looked up into stormy gray eyes.

Hawk Westbrook stood tall and sinister, staring down at her in the dim light from the old wall fixture.

"Trusting, aren't you? Leaving your door unlocked to any stranger," he commented dryly. "Well, are you ready?"

Kelcy jumped to her feet, nearly upsetting a small vase on the coffee table in front of her.

"You're going to take me?" she blurted out.

His arrogant mouth twisted in a half smile, but he left her question unanswered, as if it needed none. He just walked over to her two suitcases and picked one up.

Kelcy watched the muscles flex beneath his faded black T-shirt. In an old shirt and jeans, he looked younger, more virile, if that were possible

—almost human, touchable. Suddenly, he turned in her direction. Their eyes met.

"What's in this suitcase? Bricks?"

Kelcy blushed. "No, my art supplies are in there."

Kelcy had gathered together a few sketch pads, canvases, color markers, and her complete paint set—a vast assortment of acrylic, oil, and water-based pigments neatly organized in a hand-tooled leather case, an expensive collection that had been a Christmas present from James Miles. Her former boss had ordered three of the special sets from a salesman who regularly came into the office. One set he had sent to a relative back East, one he had given to Kelcy, and the third he had kept for himself.

She had never understood why the paint set fascinated him so, enough that he would bring it to his office and lock it in his desk every week and take it home every weekend. Granted, it was a wonderful set, and Kelcy treasured hers. But as far as she knew, James Miles was no artist and, in fact, had never broken the seal on any of his paint tubes. She had discovered this quite by chance her very last workday, the day her boss had fled town. As was usual when Kelcy ran low on certain colors, she would bring her own set into the office to purchase replacements from the available stock. This entailed writing up a stock order. By coincidence she had brought in her set just that Friday. She was in the process of checking her paint tubes when Mr. Miles returned from lunch and saw what she was doing.

Immediately, he had rushed over to question her. At first, he had seemed agitated, much to her surprise since normally Mr. Miles was a calm, soft-spoken man. But then, when she had explained, he relaxed, smiled, and tore up her stock order.

He laughed, told her the order would not be necessary, then quickly went into his own office and brought out his identical leather case, opened it, and began replacing her nearly empty tubes with his unused ones. She had been overwhelmed by his generosity.

"Why are you taking all these art supplies?" Hawk demanded, bringing her sharply back to the present.

"B-because," she stammered, "I thought I might sketch, maybe paint a bit in my spare time."

He raised one dark eyebrow sardonically. "Really? You think I'm going to allow you spare time then?" Suddenly, he laughed rather bitterly and snapped up the remaining suitcase. "You look ready, so let's go. It's about a three-hour drive from Porton up to the old house. And I can't imagine you wanting to stay in this place any longer than you'd have to. Well, come on. You'd better get moving!"

Kelcy switched off the light, adjusted her shoulder bag, and, holding fast to a small potted violet plant and a big tote bag, stepped out of the apartment, locking the door behind her. She silently vowed to speak to Hawk Westbrook as little as possible in the future, to restrict herself to yes-no responses whenever she could.

As they reached his Mercedes, she saw that all the damage had been repaired. She also saw a black-and-tan dog poking his sharply pointed nose through the half-open passenger window. The Doberman was panting loudly and showing his white, shiny teeth. He barked gruffly as his master approached.

Hawk opened the passenger door, then put Kelcy's tote bag and suitcases into the trunk.

He shot her an impatient glance. "Door's open. What are you waiting for? Get in!"

"Your dog!" She flushed nervously. "Will he jump out? I couldn't stop him if he tried. My hands are full."

"Guthrie is carefully trained, Miss Kendal. He minds better than most kids. The only time he might jump is when he's being overly friendly and hasn't been told to stay put." He gave a command to the dog. "Guthrie, backseat, stay!"

In one leap the dog landed in the back where he sprawled full length across the seat.

"I hope you like dogs, because if you don't, you might be uncomfortable."

"Oh, I do." Kelcy smiled. "We always had dogs on the farm when I grew up. We even had—" She stopped in midsentence and glanced shyly at the pavement. Already she had broken her vow. "Yes," she mumbled, "I like dogs." She reached for the car door.

Once inside, she put her shoulder bag on her lap, placing the potted violets on top of it and holding them securely between her hands, unaware of the interest that had for one fleeting second flashed across Hawk's grim face. They drove in silence for some time.

"Have you eaten?" he suddenly asked as miles of planted fields slipped by.

The silence had been so soothing that Kelcy jumped at the sound of his voice. Even Guthrie stirred in the backseat.

"I'm not hungry," she replied softly.

"And that's not what I asked you," he snapped impatiently. "Have you eaten?"

Through clenched teeth she answered, "No!"

He reached down and fumbled with the radio knob. "Then we'll stop for something at one of the hamburger joints along the way. There's a drive-in on the lakeshore that you'll enjoy." He tuned in on a ball game. "Are you interested in baseball?"

"Not especially," she said stiffly, wondering why he was asking all the questions. She knew for a fact he didn't care a stitch about her feelings.

"Well, that's a shame." He smiled. "Because I plan on listening to the game. Toronto at Milwaukee, by the way and it should be a good one. I had tickets for tonight, but I changed my mind about going and gave them to my cousin Glen. You remember him, of course, your knight in shining armor, champion of justice, and all that rot. But what was I saying? Oh, yes, it should be a good game."

Not as good as the game you play, Kelcy thought coolly as they drove out of a lovely old fishing town, the lighthouse sending its beam to the waves of Lake Michigan.

"We'll eat here," Hawk announced, pulling into a drive-in several minutes later.

It was nearing eight-thirty, growing dark, and

Kelcy could see many lights flickering along the lakefront.

Usually by this time Kelcy would have been starved, but tonight she was not interested in food. All the same, she began to wonder who was going to pay for this. She placed her pot on the floor and started digging through her shoulder bag for her wallet.

Hawk glanced at her sharply. "What are you doing now?"

"Checking to see how much money—"

"Forget that," he snapped, "and decide what you want to order. I'd like to call it in. I'll take care of the bill."

Kelcy replied stiffly, "I'd rather pay for my own meal."

"Order," he said impatiently.

Reluctantly, Kelcy looked at the menu. It was mounted on a post beside his window. She had to lean toward him to see it, and the brief closeness made her feel uneasy, disturbingly so. To cover her embarrassment, she quickly said, "I'll have that shrimp in a burger. With extra pickles and a root beer."

"Pickles?" He looked doubtful. "Humph! Is that it?"

"Yes," she said curtly, sat back, and stared out her window. Then she opened her door. "I'm going to wash my hands. The flower pot got me all dirty."

"You needn't explain," Hawk drawled lazily, making her cheeks flush.

She slammed the door.

Having stalled for as much time as possible—

anything to escape that man for even a few minutes —she headed back to the car. Suddenly aware that someone had come up behind her, she spun around.

"So you finally decided to come back," Hawk said.

She asked, "Did you think I wouldn't?"

Instantly his gray eyes blazed. Then just as quickly, his anger cooled. He smiled ruefully. "Don't think you could get away from me that easily."

Kelcy felt a cold chill run up her spine.

"And I suppose you were coming to get me!"

"Guess again. I was taking Guthrie for a walk along the rocks down there edging the beach."

Her gaze fell to the dog sitting patiently at his heel. Again his words had caused an exaggerated reaction within her, and she hated herself for the irrational response. She continued walking toward the car wondering why he had such a powerful effect on her emotions—no other man ever had.

When the tray of food arrived, Kelcy watched Hawk hand the young carhop a large bill and tell her to keep the change. Immediately, the girl broke into smiles and began treating him as if he were royalty.

Kelcy thought the girl's display was sickening, but Hawk didn't seem to mind one bit, joking with her as if they were old friends. He was obviously used to such fuss and attention. Most likely, he even expected it, Kelcy thought.

At last the girl left with a final swing of her trim hips, and Hawk began sorting through the wrapped items on the tray.

"Here you are," handing Kelcy her shrimp burger. "I hope they remembered your pickles."

"Well, I'm sure if they didn't," she replied sourly, "all you have to do is snap your fingers, and that cute carhop will slink right out here with a whole jar!"

He stared at her, genuinely surprised by her comment. Then he smiled.

# CHAPTER FIVE

"What's gotten into you, Miss Kendal?" Hawk asked.

Her pretty face glowed crimson with anger—a ridiculous anger, she realized, but nonetheless an anger. And had she not known better, which she did, she might have confused her anger with jealousy. Jealous? No way was she jealous, Kelcy told herself. How absurd!

"You didn't think that carhop was just a little overbearing?" she asked.

There was a hint of amusement in his eyes as he answered, "Not really. She's just the helpful, friendly type. A very pleasant waitress, in my opinion. But then I'm not the judge you would be with all your past waitress experience."

"Well, I do know one thing, Mr. Westbrook,"

Kelcy snapped. "I was never tipped twice the cost of the order! I believe fifteen percent is standard."

"Maybe if you'd tried smiling more, your tips might have been better," Hawk remarked coolly. "Don't worry, I won't add the cost of the meal to the amount you already owe me, if that's what you're thinking. Besides, with the special way they had to make up the order, it was a fitting reward."

Special way! Kelcy looked at him, confused. But, of course, he was referring to her simple request for pickles. Now she wished she had never heard of pickles! To her relief, he said no more and began to eat his sandwich, tossing a scrap of beef to Guthrie in the backseat. She, too, began to eat.

The shrimp burger tasted delicious despite her anger, and suddenly Kelcy found herself in a good mood, enjoying it thoroughly, just as he had said she would—the arrogant beast!

Kelcy was much more relaxed as they continued driving. In fact, she soon fell asleep.


Something warm and wet was gently rubbing her face, and Kelcy flung her eyes open in shock. What was happening? On instinct, she reached up and pushed away a large hunk of fur.

"Guthrie thought it was time you woke up, Sleeping Beauty," Hawk Westbrook said, smiling sardonically as he leaned on the open car door.

Kelcy glanced around. The car was parked on a paved driveway in front of an elegant white three-story Colonial-style house.

"I—I fell asleep?" Kelcy asked in stunned confusion.

"Now that's obvious, Miss Kendal," he replied. "Are you getting out? It's the end of the line."

His hand clamped tightly around her arm as he bent forward and, whether she liked it or not, she was being hauled from the security of the car into the foreign night air.

"Go up to the front door and wait for me there while I get your luggage," he ordered.

For a moment longer than necessary Hawk held her captive, his firm touch sending her pulses racing. Then he turned away and walked to the trunk.

From the white-boarded porch that ran the length of the house, a feminine voice called out: "Charles Hawken, is that you out there? My dear, what a pleasant surprise!"

Kelcy spun around to see a plump figure silhouetted in the doorway. The woman had a lovely head of silver curls and was wrapped in a light rose shawl. Her hand waved gracefully in a friendly welcome.

"Yes, Aunt Jenna, it's me, and I know I'm early," Hawk shouted from his post behind the car as he gathered the bags and slammed the trunk tightly. "I'll explain later."

"Heavens! You must be tired. Well, hurry and come in then . . . although I don't know what I'll feed you since the cook's gone home for the evening. Is that Mrs. Cranden with you?"

As Hawk came even with Kelcy, he shot her a warning glance. She looked at her bags, the way he held them, and half expected him to hand them to her to carry, but he didn't.

"Now, where the devil did that dog run off to?" he snapped, scanning the grounds.

"When your aunt was holding the door open, he went inside," Kelcy informed him.

"Oh. Well, are you going to stand there all night?"

"N-no, of course not," Kelcy stammered. "Can I at least take my shoulder bag and plant from the car?"

He sighed deeply. "Get them and hurry up!"

Silently she reentered the car, collected her things, and followed Hawk up the pavement to the porch steps. There were brass pots of red-and-white geraniums interlaced with strings of ivy lining the walk. Lovely, Kelcy thought with an artist's admiration and realized that they made her tiny violet plant look sick.

"Hawk, I'm so glad you decided to come," Aunt Jenna was saying. And then she stopped, her blue eyes for the first time seeing the girl lagging behind her tall, handsome nephew. "You brought someone else with you, not Mrs. Cranden?"

"Ahh, this is . . ." He jerked his head in Kelcy's direction. "Well, let's go inside first. We ate on the way up, so don't bother about food. Are our rooms ready, Jenna?"

Having stepped through the doorway, Kelcy gazed about her in awe. It was as if she had stepped back in time, and the discovery was magic. For the house was apparently filled with antiques and also exquisite replicas, all of them examples of quality and fine craftsmanship. Polished woods, old brass finishes, and glass could be seen everywhere. The place promised to be so extraordinarily beautiful and interesting, Kelcy felt that she could spend a year here and still never see enough of it.

Hawk's words broke her spell. "This is Miss Kendal, Aunt Jenna." He deposited her bags on the floor and was now dragging Kelcy into a blue carpeted room past a handsome hall tree of dark maple. "She's going to be working as my secretary while I'm here."

Jenna looked hopelessly confused as she hung her shawl on one of the brass hooks and followed them in. "But, Hawk, what happened to Mrs. Cranden? I thought she was your private secretary. She didn't quit, did she?"

"No, of course not, Jenna. But I could hardly expect her to come up here for the summer, could I?"

"Oh, I see. I do see, yes." Jenna smiled wistfully. "Then you are planning to work up here! I thought it too good to be true. Well, Miss Kendal, welcome! Do you think you'll like it here, dear?"

"Yes, it's beautiful."

"She doesn't have to like it, Jenna. She's here to work, nothing more!" Hawk cut in sharply.

Jenna gazed disapprovingly at her nephew. "Hawk, what's gotten into you? You're being unnecessarily rude to this lovely girl!" Jenna smiled at Kelcy. "And you are lovely, my dear. My nephew has been known to be ill-tempered. The family is used to him. But I can see that you're not. Don't let him upset you."

Kelcy glanced down at the soft carpet beneath her old leather sandals. So Hawk hadn't told his aunt about the car damages or why he had brought her here. All at once she felt sick at the thought that he would. She trembled, unhappy at the idea of this kindly woman believing she was a thief.

"What is it, Miss Kendal?" Jenna asked. "Hawk, I do think this girl is ill!"

"No, please, I'm fine," Kelcy said, though she felt simply awful. "I'm just tired."

Hawk was suddenly at her side. ''Well, are you ill?" His voice was sharp. Sharper than she had ever heard it before. The sharpness of anxiety.

"No!"

He chose to ignore her answer and looked at her closely. "You are a bit flushed. She was, after all, just released from the hospital today, Aunt Jenna."

Jenna took the news with shocked disbelief. "What did you say, Hawk? Released from the hospital? Oh, what could you be thinking of! How insensitive to shove that poor girl into a car and drag her all the way up here. But then I can't say your actions surprise me!" She put her arm around Kelcy protectively. "Poor dear, of course, you're tired. Hawk can be such a brute at times! I'll show you to your room so that you can rest."

Hawk shrugged. "Aunt Jenna, stop fussing and let the housekeeper settle her in." He glanced around. "Where is everyone?"

"Elsewhere!" Jenna responded crossly. "We weren't expecting you tonight."

"Is that how things are with the staff you hired? So they come and go as they please! Well, that will soon change."

With a sigh, Jenna patted Kelcy's shoulder, then

turned to face her nephew. "I beg your pardon, young man. This is a well-run house with trustworthy employees. They've been working almost round the clock for the past two days to get everything in order for your arrival. Since you weren't expected until tomorrow, I gave them the time off. You wouldn't be questioning my capabilities, would you?"

"You know better than that, Jenna," he answered, exasperated. "But you do tend to be too soft and let people take advantage of you. Look how you've taken to Miss Kendal. You know nothing about her."

"Well, I sure know about you, Hawk, and I know, too, that you wouldn't bring anyone into this house who wasn't okay. For heaven's sake, Hawk, stop upsetting this girl! She looks dead tired!"

Kelcy felt awkward and ashamed. Again she had become the center of a Westbrook family argument. She wished she could run out of the house, away from Hawk Westbrook. But she just stood there, trembling, her hands gripping her small clay pot of violets, for she knew there would be no escaping him!

"Well, perhaps she does look tired," Hawk conceded grudgingly. "Where should I put her things?"

Jenna smiled at her small victory. "That out-of-the-way room at the far end of the house, Hawk. I had thought Mrs. Cranden would like the privacy. But maybe we can arrange something else for Miss Kendal. There is that large, airy room upstairs that we could consider."

"I'm sure the room you have prepared will be

fine," Hawk drawled. "Miss Kendal is my secretary, not the Queen of England, after all."

"Hawk, really!" Jenna said. "Don't be so crude. Now let's show her the room."

While Hawk got Kelcy's bags, Jenna guided her to a door near the back of the house. Jenna turned the handle as Hawk reappeared with the luggage.

"Here it is," the older woman said.

Kelcy walked in. She loved the wide plank floor covered with braided rugs, the fireplace, the canopy bed fringed with lace, the pine rocking chair, and the other furnishings.

"You can put your little plant on the dresser by the window." Jenna smiled. "I'm so glad you like flowers, dear. Mrs. Cranden—well, I'm not sure she likes much of anything. I hope you'll be comfortable here. It is a bit old-fashioned, I know, but it's the style of the house. Perhaps we should leave now, Hawk, so that Miss—what is your first name, dear? I hate to be so formal."

"Kelcy."

"Oh, how lovely! Teutonic, isn't it? And something to do with water, I think. I make a study of these things as a sort of hobby, you see. Now what was I saying? Oh, yes, Kelcy should get some rest, Hawk. We wouldn't want her quitting on us before she even begins work. Good night then, Kelcy. If you need anything, just ask."

Before she left, Jenna took the pot from Kelcy and placed it on a lace doily atop the dresser. Then, after one last look at the little flowers, she shuffled through the doorway, smiling contentedly to herself.

Hawk glanced around the room. "I see they re-stained the shutters in here," he said absently. "Does it suit you?"

"What color were they before?" Kelcy asked. As if he cared whether anything suited her.

"Huh?"

"The shutters. Oh, I see, you didn't wonder if they suited me. You meant the room! Well, it's fine."

"Better than you're used to, anyway," he re-marked cuttingly.

Trying to ignore his haughty comment, she asked:

"Are you going to tell your aunt why I'm here?"

His face grew hard. "I'm not sure. For now, no. I don't want to upset her. And for whatever the reason, she's taken a liking to you." He walked to the door. "Get some rest. I want you alert and ready to begin work in the morning."

The door closed tightly behind him.

A little later, after Kelcy had unpacked her things and was settled comfortably between the cool, crisp sheets, she listened to the gentle night sounds outside her window, absorbing the stillness of the dark room. Suddenly it was shattered by a knock at the door. Bolting up, she switched on the nightstand lamp and grabbed wildly for her robe.

Kelcy froze as Hawk Westbrook strode, uncere-moniously and uninvited, through her doorway. She was still in bed, her robe flung over her pajamas.

What a nerve! Kelcy was aghast. What did he mean, barging in here like that?

His gray eyes regarded her smilingly. "My aunt

wished to know if you had settled in. I see that you have."

Aware that he was making her uncomfortable, and roguishly enjoying it, he walked closer to her bed, taking a small thin book from one of his pockets. He held it out to her.

"Jenna asked me to give this to you. It's a short history of the area, including sections on the nearby mill. She thought you might enjoy reading it."

Kelcy reached out to take it. "Yes, thank her," she said tensely. Her heart had never raced so fast. She thought it might burst. As she lowered her eyes, bending her head slightly to examine the book, her hands trembled.

"Feeling better, Kelcy?" Hawk asked softly.

She blinked, glancing up to meet his eyes, not sure that she had heard him correctly.

The light from the lamp gleamed on his bent head, burnishing the tousled dark hair. At that moment she longed to stroke it gently, and just as quickly got upset by the idea. What on earth would make her think such outrageous things? she chided herself severely. What was happening to her? She must be going mad. It was this place—this beautifully welcoming place. The magic it brewed had a way of seeping through to the very bone.

She nodded. "I'm feeling much better."

"Good, because you start work at eight," he answered in that deep and dangerously magnetic tone. "You can eat breakfast with the staff in the kitchen at seven and then meet me out front. I'll take you to the mill myself." His voice grew cold again. "And after office hours, I expect you to stay in your room, out of sight. Unless Aunt Jenna needs you for something. I told her she can count on you for errands and the like."

If there had been any magic floating through the air, Charles Hawken Westbrook had wasted no time in blasting it away.

"Like a prisoner!" she said.

"If the shoe fits, Miss Kendal . . ." he flung back at her.

And with that he left her.

Kelcy tossed and turned and fumed for some time before she fell asleep.

# CHAPTER SIX

After a brisk morning shower, Kelcy nervously slipped into some white slacks and a red-and-white-print shirt. She swept her hair up into a cool knot, allowing the slightest feathering of bangs to brush her forehead. She hoped she looked all right for work.

Breakfast, she learned upon reaching the modern kitchen, was an informal affair. Kelcy introduced herself to the cook, a plump, curly-haired, middle-aged, friendly woman named Mrs. Meinert, who spoke with a heavy German accent. They exchanged a few pleasantries before the woman handed her a plate of scrambled eggs, toast, and bacon and motioned for her to take a chair at the round oak table.

Kelcy was almost through eating when a man and a woman entered the kitchen by way of the

61

back door. They both glanced at her with interest before helping themselves to cups of coffee and sitting down.

"A new face," said the smiling blond, blue-eyed woman, who was in her late thirties. "I'm Sue Gill and this bearded wonder is my husband, Brad."

Brad smiled, too. He did indeed have a neatly trimmed red beard with a thick mass of red curls on his head to match. "You wouldn't by any chance be here to apply for that stable-hand job I've got advertised? Now I know all about that women's lib jazz. Sue badgers me with it all the time." He laughed. "But I specifically stated I wanted a teenage boy who can also help with the haying."

Kelcy said, "Well, Mr. Gill, I'll have you know that in my carefree days on my parents' farm I could swing a mean bale of hay, perhaps as well as any teenage boy. But I've long since retired from that line of work. I'm Kelcy Kendal, Mr. Westbrook's temporary secretary."

"Then it's true!" Sue Gill said as the cook brought over their eggs and bacon. "He is planning to work up here from the old mill office. Mrs. Dole, his dear aunt, said he might be coming. She'll like that. Now she'll be able to do a bit more traveling. She loves to go with her friends, but she hasn't done too much of that because of her 'family duty,' as she puts it. Oh, by the way, just for the record, I'm in charge of the housekeeping here, if you have any complaints. Mrs. Meinert doesn't need anyone to manage her. She's near perfect. But some of my part-time college girls surely do. And Brad manages the stables and supervises the ground workers. We live a few miles down the road with our three kids. Welcome!"

"Thank you," Kelcy said. "I'm glad to meet both of you. And I'm glad the countryside here is so lovely."

"Yeah, it's nice up here," Brad said, absently gazing out the window. "The ideal place. And for me, it's the ideal job, too. I get to train and work with horses I could never afford. And I'm paid good to boot. If you ride or would like to learn, Sue will be glad to take you out on the trails after work. Those horses Mr. Westbrook has love attention. I don't know the man too well yet, but what I do know I like. He's fair and honest and sure can handle a horse—and not manhandle them either like some of the wealthy jerks I've worked for in the past."

"He probably likes animals more than people," Kelcy said suddenly, without thinking.

Brad laughed. "Probably. Some guys are like that."

"And you oughta know, dear," Sue popped up. "You're one of them."

"I guess I am, honey," he responded. "Well, so don't forget, Kelcy. Come on down to the stables whenever you get the time."

Kelcy smiled to herself knowingly. Hawk Westbrook was not about to allow her any free time. After work, he had ordered her to stay in her room like a naughty child. If he caught her near his precious horses, he'd probably keep her on bread and water for a month.

Ah, but she was only going to be there three

weeks, and then Glen would rescue her, she reminded herself happily.

To Brad and Sue, however, Kelcy just said, "Well, we'll see," not wishing to admit to these nice people Hawk Westbrook had placed her under house arrest. She glanced at her watch. It was twenty to eight, and she wanted to be early. "It's so nice to have met all of you, but this being my first day, I don't want to be late. So I'd better be off."

In unison the three said good-bye and wished her luck. Kelcy walked through the kitchen door onto a wood-decked patio flanked by flower boxes. Then she took a stone path that led to the front yard. It was amazing, she thought to herself, how everyone here was so warm and friendly, with the exception of the head of the house himself, Hawk Westbrook. If they'd met under different circumstances, would he have been so openly hostile, or would he, too, have been pleasant, even charming? And what would have happened then?

Kelcy was pondering those very questions when she spied Guthrie sprawled lengthwise under the shade of a maple tree. The moment he saw her, he jumped up and bounded over.

"No, Guthrie," Kelcy yelled, holding out her hands to keep him from leaping up. "You'll get mud all over my white slacks and I'll have to go back and change."

She managed to avoid his friendly attack and grabbed him by the collar, taking him with her to the porch stairs.

"Now, Guthrie," Kelcy scolded the dog lightheartedly while she bent down and gave him a big hug, "go off and play. I'm waiting for your master."

She watched the dog's big brown eyes flicker with interest, almost as if he had understood. And after some romping and barking, he suddenly tore off in the direction of the woods.

Kelcy sat down on a nearby porch chair and waited. Within moments Guthrie came trotting back, half-carrying, half-dragging a dried-out branch. Smiling, she got the distinct impression that Guthrie wanted to play catch. So why not? She decided, walking over to meet him.

"Okay, boy, but let's just take a piece of this." Kelcy broke off a short stick and tossed it across the lawn. Guthrie raced over, snatching it out of mid-air, and pranced around.

"Good boy, now bring it here," Kelcy coaxed.

He came within several feet of her. But when she tried to take the stick from his mouth, he skillfully avoided her hand.

"Well, you've got this fetch game half right, you overgrown pup." She smiled. "But don't think I'm chasing after you."

After one or two more tries to corner the dog, she gave up and went back to the porch, this time to sit on the stairs instead of in a chair. The sleek animal was thoroughly enjoying himself, chewing, shaking, and bringing the stick to just within her reach, then racing off.

While she watched his amusing antics, Kelcy happened to notice the leather strap on her right sandal was twisted. In her early-morning nervousness, she supposed she had buckled the thing wrong, which would never do. For already she could feel a blister forming on her foot. When she undid the strap, Guthrie darted over. Before she realized his intentions, he snapped up her sandal in his mouth and tore off down the drive at top speed.

"Guthrie!" Kelcy yelled. "Bring that back!"

She was on her feet in seconds, dashing after him. The dog was not stopping. Instead, he turned sharply onto a stone path heading into the woods. She followed in hot pursuit.

When she could no longer see him, Kelcy stopped for a moment, unsure if she should continue with this mad chase. Her breath was coming rapidly and she felt a little woozy. After all, she had been warned by that hospital doctor to rest and take things easy for the next few weeks—but still she wanted her sandal! Just then she thought she heard something stirring in the distant brush.

She smiled. Maybe Guthrie had had enough fun and was coming back. Kelcy listened more closely. Somewhere in the background she could also hear the sound of running water. A stream? A river? In the next second there was a loud splash.

"Oh, no! Not that dog with my sandal!" Kelcy sighed heavily. She took off toward the sound in a flash, oblivious to everything, forgetting all caution.

She hadn't gone far when the path twisted sharply. Kelcy had been concentrating on her footing, for the going was hard with only one sandal. As she blindly rounded the bend, she did not see the tall figure moving closer. Not until she felt the violent collision did she realize what had happened.

When Hawk Westbrook reached out instinctively to steady her, his two strong hands firmly gripping her arms, Kelcy's heart leapt to her throat.

"And just where were you going in such a hurry, Miss Kendal?" he demanded.

He faced her, looking big, angry, tough in his jeans and riding boots.

"I was chasing Guthrie. He stole my sandal and —and I didn't expect anyone else to be out here, so I wasn't watching where I was going. You didn't see him, did you? He came down this path."

To Kelcy's surprise, Hawk Westbrook laughed. "That dog. He can be a real pest at times. Especially when he's in high spirits. You're lucky your foot wasn't in your shoe. Which, by the way, is something I'd like to know—just why wasn't your foot in your sandal, Miss Kendal?"

Instead of answering his question, she said, "Guthrie's your dog, Mr. Westbrook. And for all your bragging about his obedience training, I surely couldn't see any sign of it!"

"Guthrie minds his master, Miss Kendal. That's all that's required from him. Now if you think I've got all morning, to waste while you chase through the woods after Guthrie—I haven't. I'm a busy man. There's work to be done."

Kelcy shook her head. "There's no use talking to you. All right, I'll forget the sandal. Tell me what you want me to do and leave it at that."

The merest glimmer of a smile touched his arrogant mouth. "You learn fast. I'll see if I can get Guthrie to give up your sandal, and we'll go." He looked over his shoulder and yelled a harsh command to the wind.

All at once Guthrie came bounding out of the bushes and headed toward his master.

Hawk turned back to Kelcy. "Aren't you going to ask where he was?"

"No," she answered.

He began to laugh. "Fine. Now I'm taking you up to the old mill office—where you should have been fifteen minutes ago."

But first he asked Guthrie to drop the sandal. After looking it over for damage, Hawk handed it to her. The sole and leather straps were wet from Guthrie's saliva and slightly marred by tooth marks, but the sandal was wearable.

She leaned against the nearest tree and slipped it on, buckling it properly this time. "Okay, I'm ready to go to work. And thank you," she replied evenly.

"Don't thank me. I didn't want you up here at all. Save your gratitude for Glen." He started walking down the path from which Guthrie had emerged only moments before.

Kelcy watched him go, his dog at his heel, and thought about what he had said. Suddenly she felt cold and rubbed her arms where he had gripped them earlier.

"Come on, Miss Kendal," he called without looking back.

She went quickly, fearing his impatience. He had stopped to pet Guthrie, waiting for her to catch up. His reference to Glen had surprised her. Did Hawk know more about his cousin's activities on Friday night than he was letting on?

He scowled at her feet. "You'd better get a sturdier pair of shoes for working up here when you go shopping with Jenna tomorrow," he said. "And since Guthrie all but trashed those, charge them to my account"

Kelcy was surprised. No one had told her she was going shopping with his aunt tomorrow. Even if he was the boss, he didn't have to be so dictatorial about it—about everything! His words, his warning, his uppity, condescending tone reminded her so much of the way Bess used to speak to her that she responded in her own insolent style.

"Yes, sir, Mr. Westbrook! Anything you say, sir, Mr. Westbrook!"

"Don't be impertinent, Miss Kendal. You have nothing to gain by it and everything to lose," Hawk told her.

"I was not being impertinent!"

Kelcy was unaware of the picture she made at that moment, her green eyes deliciously provocative, wisps of her hair gently stirring in the warm breeze. Hawk Westbrook's hard eyes softened briefly.

Then he smiled mockingly. "The work I have waiting for you in the office should take some of that sassy, cheeky energy out of you in a quick hurry, young lady."

They were facing each other on the narrow path, with a soft wind swirling about. Even the birds were still, and a chill of expectation touched Kelcy's spine. The air was electric. She would have been happy to slap Hawk's face.

Instead, she told him pleasantly, "I can't wait to get started, just show me the way."

He silently led her along the path to an opening where a sturdy wooden bridge—wide enough for two cars to cross—spanned a smallish river.

On the other side of the bridge stood a large stone building with tall windows and huge wooden doors built solidly along the water's edge. The bridge led straight to those doors, making it the only front access to the mill. Beneath the bridge, fastened to the lower half of the east wall, was a working water wheel, turning slowly, steadily.

The sight was breathtaking. Kelcy felt as if she had stepped into an old fairy tale. There were pines on either side of the building, and nearby were many shrubs and flowers. Best of all, there were several ducks in the water.

"It's perfect," she said softly.

Hawk strode up beside her. "Perfect for what? A prison? A fortress? A haven? A hideout? A country memory? What, Miss Kendal?"

If he was baiting her, she wasn't biting. "A mill office, Mr. Westbrook." She smiled faintly. "Although it seems so secluded. Did they actually do a thriving business out here? I mean, surely a farmer couldn't take a grain wagon down that path we just walked."

Hawk laughed. "No, the main road comes in here from the south." He pointed to a paved drive nearly hidden from view by trees.

"Oh, I see."

"It's the original building and landscape with a few modern touches added—like electricity and heat," he went on to inform her.

"And that stone sign that says HAWK'S MILL.

That has to be new. But where did you find stones to match so perfectly, as if they were mortared to the mill from the beginning?"

He laughed again. "They were. Believe it or not, that is the original name of this mill. Are you surprised to discover I'm not as egotistic as you thought? The early farmer's here noticed that each spring the hawks came to nest on the roofs of their barns. So it seemed natural to name this place after the hawk. You know, this was the only grain mill in the area, and all the local farmers brought in their grains for grinding or surplus sale. They shipped their goods by river out to the bay where they were loaded onto lake vessels. Back then it was a very successful, efficient operation."

He had stopped talking now, apparently finished with what he had to say.

"That's very interesting," Kelcy said when the silence seemed to drag on endlessly.

"Yes, isn't it?" he replied derisively. "But enough stalling. Come along and I'll put you to work."

She followed him silently. When she stepped through the doors, it was like entering another world. There were grain sacks and grain vats and other items that gave an air of authenticity to the place. And in the center was a big staircase.

Kelcy looked up. "Where will I be working?"

"Up there on the second floor. Follow me."

She did.

Most of the space on the second floor was taken up by Hawk's huge office, furnished with rich leather furniture, a massive oak desk, book-lined shelves, and various electronic gadgets scattered about. Next to it was a smaller room with a file cabinet, a desk, a phone, a bathroom, and word-processing equipment. The two offices were separated by large glass windows with blinds.

After Kelcy had looked around, Hawk walked to a door in the bigger office. He opened it, and she saw that it led to a third room, a most intimidating place.

"For starters, you'll be working in here, Miss Kendal, the brain center of our outfit. These very expensive computers, two of them, to be exact, tap into my main office in the city. So do these phone lines. Your first assignment will be to program those stacks of data in that file cabinet." He pointed to a five-drawer cabinet and handed her a thick instruction book.

Kelcy stared at the book in shock. He had to be kidding. She had never worked with such sophisticated equipment in her life, and the task he wanted her to carry out would even be hard for someone with experience.

"I know nothing about these computers, Mr. Westbrook," she told him, glaring at the instruction book in confusion. "I've only worked with a very simple one. You can't expect me to—"

Hawk grabbed her wrist, forcing her to sit in the chair facing him. "I expect you to follow my orders. The salesman I spoke to from the computer company assured me a ten-year-old child could operate this thing."

A ten-year-old genius, maybe, Kelcy thought. "Well, if you'll show me how this thing works—"

"That's what the instruction book is for," was his cool reply, danger glinting in his steely eyes. "Put some of your energy into your work, Miss Kendal. That's what you're here for!" He rigidly strode to the door, turning back suddenly when he reached it. "I'll be out riding all morning. Take any messages that come through. And Miss Kendal, I expect to see some progress when I get back."

Once she had heard him leave the mill, Kelcy slumped back in her chair and closed her eyes, sighing deeply. How would she ever get through the next three weeks without cracking? she wondered gloomily. If only she could contact Glen to let him know what a ruthless cousin he had. But he already knew that, didn't he?

"'Miss Kendal, I expect to see some progress when I get back,'" Kelcy mocked him out loud. "You bet you will, Mr. Westbrook, sir!" she added playfully, opening the computer manual and taking a thick file from the cabinet. "And if I mess up this expensive machine, it's your own fault!"

Hawk Westbrook meant to punish her. So it would seem. Yet Kelcy could not help but feel there was more behind it than just the money for those car damages. After all, he was a very wealthy man. And, according to the figures on these company reports she was reading, growing wealthier by the minute. But if money did not motivate his ruthless behavior, what did?

Perhaps it was his pride, she guessed. He was upset that someone had dared to steal his property, challenge his authority. Anyone who dared to cross him would pay and pay dearly. That thought made her shudder, for she had been the only one caught. Poor Glen, when he confessed, she thought now as she began to match up the buttons on the computer with the diagrams in the book. Poor Glen! She shook her head. What was she thinking? He had gotten her into this trouble in the first place. How could she waste her sympathy on him?

Three weeks seemed an incredibly long way off. And since there was no chance of settling things before then, she had no option but to try her best to please her boss. If there was such a thing as pleasing him.

# CHAPTER SEVEN

It was hard to believe that the morning had passed so quickly. Once Kelcy had studied the opening pages of the computer manual thoroughly —and begun punching in the data—all time was lost. She found it tiring at first. But as she became more familiar with the machine, the work grew easier. She felt she was making a nice start at transferring the information from the files into the computer. And she derived a certain satisfaction from the achievement.

At one point Kelcy had been tempted to pick up the phone and ask for help from one of the employees at the main office. But an unfamiliar shyness had held her back, and so far she felt she was doing adequately by herself.

"Kelcy?"

Taken by surprise, she looked around, dropping

the file she had been skimming before transferring it to the machine. "Oh, Sue, you startled me!"

"Sorry, Kelcy, but it's no wonder you're so jumpy. It's nearly one and you haven't had lunch yet. Mrs. Dole will accuse me of neglecting my duties if you don't take a break now and eat. Come on, I brought you a fruit salad, baked trout, rolls, and juice. I remember you don't seem to like coffee."

Kelcy got up and followed Sue to her office desk where the food tray sent out a tempting aroma. "It smells delicious. I'll just duck into the bathroom over there to wash up. I'll be right back."

Sue was uncovering the dishes when Kelcy reentered. "You like trout, don't you?" the housekeeper asked.

"I love all types of fish," Kelcy answered.

"Good, because we serve a lot of fish up here. Brad and my boys are out on the lake every weekend so you'd almost have to like fish to survive."

"Umm, this is great!" Kelcy replied, having just swallowed a forkful of trout. "I didn't know if I was supposed to come to the kitchen for lunch or not. In fact, Mr. Westbrook never mentioned anything about lunch. I thought perhaps I could just make a sandwich and eat it here after today."

Sue frowned. "You'll do nothing of the kind. Of course, you come to the house at noon. I suppose he didn't tell you because it slipped his mind. Anyway, he couldn't have meant for you to starve."

Kelcy smiled to herself thinking that he'd probably meant just that, but she said nothing about it to

Sue. She just ate some more trout. Then she began to worry about all the files in the other room.

"I hope you don't mind if I continue working while I eat. Mr. Westbrook gave me a lot to do." Kelcy smiled at Sue.

"Whew! He's really got you trained to the whip. Well, today you're not working during lunch. And don't let him turn you into one of those machines like the efficient Mrs. Cranden. His dear aunt warned us about her. At first we were expecting her, you know. Jenna had us prepared for the worst. But I'm sure glad he brought you instead. I think she might have made me a nervous wreck."

Kelcy laughed. "It could be the poor woman's just misunderstood. I haven't known Mr. Westbrook very long, but I do know he's very demanding. Perhaps some of his dictatorial, lordly attitude has rubbed off on her."

"Perhaps," Sue sighed. "I really don't know. Well, just enjoy a nice long lunch and take it easy. I'll let you in on a little secret. Jenna said she didn't think Hawk came up here to work, anyway."

"No, I guess not. That's why he brought me—to do his work for him."

Sue smiled slyly. "I don't think you caught my meaning."

But before Kelcy could ask her exactly what she meant, Hawk Westbrook walked through the door, followed by a sandy-haired man dressed casually in navy pants and short-sleeved shirt and carrying a briefcase. The stranger loosened his striped tie and smiled at the two women.

Hawk nodded to Sue. "Hello, Mrs. Gill. I just

saw Brad up at the stable, and I believe he was looking for you. Something about a teacher's meeting. He wanted to know what time it started."

"Oh, gee, is that tonight?" She put her hand to her forehead. "Thanks for reminding me. Summer session begins next week. 'Bye, Kelcy, I gotta run. Bring your dishes to the kitchen after work. Hawk, why didn't you tell her we eat at noon? The poor girl was starving!"

For a brief second, his gray eyes rested on Kelcy, and there was a spark in them that made her uneasy. What was he thinking?

She quickly swallowed some juice and put down her glass. "That's okay, Sue. Now I know."

The stranger cleared his throat. "Aren't you going to introduce me to this lovely lady, C.H.?"

Sue was on her way out and looked back. "Since you already know me, you must mean Kelcy Kendal, Hawk's new secretary, Mr. Sawyer," she playfully said. "Well, bye all!" With a tiny wave, she disappeared from sight.

Heath Sawyer smiled after he introduced himself to Kelcy. "I suppose it's Mrs.——"

She laughed softly. "No, actually not. It's Miss."

He seemed to like the news. "Good, and how are you managing here so far?"

"Very well, thank you." She watched him open his briefcase and take out a thin folder.

He addressed Hawk. "Now you want me to show her how to program these computers, right, C.H.?" Then he turned to Kelcy. "Okay, Miss Kendal, just give me a minute or two to test them out, and we can begin when you're ready."

She looked perplexed. Begin what? she asked herself. Who was this Heath Sawyer, anyway, one of Westbrook's assistants whom she would be working with? And why on earth would Hawk want him to show her anything? She had already begun to program the files. If nothing else, this should be interesting, Kelcy thought as she followed the two men into the computer room.

Heath Sawyer briefly glanced through his folder, then took a seat in front of the keyboard. Flicking on buttons, he slid over to the file cabinet, randomly selected one file from the top drawer and with long, nimble fingers started punching in data.

He stopped abruptly and gazed at the screen. "Why am I getting a repeat code as if it were already filed?" he said mostly to himself. He cleared it and tried once more with the same results. "What's going on here? C'mon, C.H., and look at this." Heath punched up the memory, gazing at the screen. "Well, I'll be—this file is in, neatly coded and all. You're pulling my leg, C.H., you don't need my help!"

"What's the joke, Sawyer?" Hawk lifted a cynical eyebrow. "I know you said this computer does everything but make coffee. However, it sure as hell doesn't program itself."

"Sure doesn't, but someone has!" Heath looked at Hawk, puzzled. Then they both turned to stare at Kelcy. "Did you by any chance do this, my dear?" Heath asked.

Kelcy's heart gave an unpleasant lurch. "I did what Mr. Westbrook told me to do. I created a file on the computer. But I didn't finish. I still have a lot more to do."

"What!" Hawk's voice was a whiplash of astonishment. "You said you didn't know anything about computers. Check it, Sawyer. See if she's telling the truth."

Heath Sawyer took out several more files, punched buttons, checked and rechecked the data, then leaned back in his chair and scratched his chin. "She sure is telling the truth," he replied. "See for yourself." He glanced at Kelcy. "I don't know why you told C.H. you don't know anything about computers. You've worked on them before, Miss Kendal. You must have!"

"Just a very small basic one where I used to work. Nothing like this complicated thing. Did I do something wrong? I tried to follow the instruction manual to the letter."

Heath laughed. "No, I wouldn't say you did anything wrong. I mean, I can't believe you did all this in one morning. I just installed the equipment yesterday. Normally, it would take someone several days to learn the machine and do what you've done so far."

Hawk stirred restlessly. "Well, you did say a ten-year-old could operate this thing, Sawyer."

"I said it, sure, C.H. But when I'm out to make a sale, I say a lot of things I don't mean." He walked over to Kelcy. "Uh, Miss Kendal, here's my card. I'm vice president of Sawyer Computer. We're based in Chicago. If you ever want a job with my company, just give me a call. I'll top any salary C.H. is paying you."

Kelcy was silent. There was nothing she could say to that. She held the card between her fingers and swallowed hard.

Without warning, the card was whisked from her grasp and Hawk Westbrook tore it in two. "She's got a job here, Sawyer," he stated gruffly, "and she'd better remember that!"

Heath Sawyer looked very uncomfortable. "Well, I didn't mean to offend you, Westbrook. I just thought—forget it. It doesn't look like I'm needed here. She has everything well under control." He looked back at the computer. "Maybe, as long as I'm here, I'll show you how to modem that. It can be a bit confusing at first, Miss Kendal, unless you've already mastered that, too."

Kelcy stared at him in dismay. "I'm sorry, I don't even know what that means."

"It's a telephone hookup that transfers the info from this computer to one at the main office. It also works in reverse," Hawk told her.

"Right," Heath agreed, "that's about it. So C.H. could just as easily have had his main-office staff program these files and he could have pulled out any data he wanted from here, but obviously he didn't want to do it that way. Of course, then you also have the originals right here. But there were probably copies of this stuff at his main office, too."

As Heath's words sank in, so did Kelcy's suspicions. "Is that right?" she replied woodenly. "In other words, it's possible all the information in the files I punched in could already be on the mainframe computer." If that was the case, she hated Hawk Westbrook more than ever!

Bemused, Heath shook his head. "I didn't mean to imply that at all. I was just making a general comment to alert you to the way this works. I doubt if C.H. would let you waste your time doing programming that was already done, huh, C.H. Help me out here."

"No." Hawk spoke softly, but his voice was as hard as tempered steel. "What would be the point, Miss Kendal, of my having you do tedious work another one of my employees has already done? You must be a bit paranoid. Those files contain new figures just released last week. I haven't even finished checking through them yet."

Kelcy still didn't trust her new boss. But she merely said, "Just how does this modem thing work, Mr. Sawyer?"

Heath was happy to be demonstrating his product. In no time, he ran through the steps, one by one, showing her which buttons to press to automatically dial up the main computer hundreds of miles away. It was easy and fast, and it made data available on a twenty-four-hour basis.

"So if you feel like working odd hours, it's great," Heath said. "I know C.H. likes to. Well, I guess that's about it." He smiled at Kelcy. "Maybe I should read these manuals more closely. They're actually not that hard to follow. And, remember, our office number is in the phone book if you have any questions—or any desire to change jobs."

"Which she doesn't," Hawk added from behind them.

"Okay, I get the point, Westbrook. I wouldn't like to lose her either if I were you. Treasures are hard to find."

"You might say this one was forced on me," Hawk said moodily.

Heath got up and packed up his briefcase. "All I can say is you're a lucky man then, C.H. Well, if you have any trouble with the computers, let me know. I'll stop in at your city offices to double-check things on that end on my way home."

After Heath Sawyer had gone, Hawk strode into his office and shut the door. Kelcy finished her lunch. She swallowed her anger with the last of her juice. So she had been forced on him, had she? What a curious expression to use—for he had agreed to Glen's idea quite willingly, she remembered. And why such bitterness—such resentment— toward her? Her mind was a whirlpool of confused thoughts. The one uppermost being that she disliked Mr. Charles Hawken Westbrook intensely. He had expected her to fail at the job he had given her. That was obvious, for he had called in his computer expert even before he had checked back with her to see how she was coping. Well, she had shown him —had she ever!

Hawk Westbrook might not like her as a person, she thought more than a bit victoriously, but as a secretary he had to admit she was good—darn good!

The next morning, Kelcy drove Mrs. Dole to the town of Fish Creek built along the bay. Hawk's aunt wanted to explore the quaint art colony and do a little shopping, she had said on the scenic drive there. Jenna's car was a compact, easy to manipulate through tourist traffic and into parking spaces, she found, having parked in a crowded lot near the water's edge.

To their right only a few yards away was the entrance to a white, clapboard-sided restaurant. On its open terrace were a dozen or more wrought-iron tables topped by colorful umbrellas. Unfortunately, there were no diners taking advantage of the lovely view today for the sky was overcast and the wind brisk.

"It's nearing eleven, Kelcy," Hawk's aunt said as she glanced at her watch. "Perhaps we should eat now before the tourist crowd arrives."

Kelcy smiled. "I expect you'll want to eat inside, too. I know the weatherman said no rain, but he could be wrong, Mrs. Dole."

"You're so right, Kelcy. This weather is miserable. One day hot, the next day cold. And please stop that 'Mrs. Dole' foolishness. Call me Jenna, or better yet, Auntie Jen, like the boys used to call me before they grew up. I sort of miss that, you know. Glen was the one who started that. Hawk tells me you and Glen are good friends. He's a nice, friendly lad."

Kelcy was unsure which statement had surprised her more. She could never call this dear lady Auntie Jen; Hawk would have a fit if he heard that. As for his telling his aunt she was Glen's friend—what was the point?

There was a long pause before Kelcy said, "If

you're certain it won't be too informal, I'll call you Jenna."

"Oh, my, no, I insist. Why, I think of you as one of the family already."

"But I'm not really, Mrs.—Jenna. I just work for Mr. Westbrook, you must remember . . . temporarily," she added cautiously.

Jenna smiled knowingly. "Hmm, now don't be too sure of that. He did say when I asked him how your first day went that you are one exceptional girl. Then he mumbled something about Glen that I didn't quite catch and said he was going out for a long walk. Why ever do you look so surprised, Kelcy? Hawk would never hire anyone he thought unsuitable."

Unless she were forced on him, Kelcy thought silently. She felt it was definitely time to change the subject. "It might be better if we did eat now. Business is picking up," she said as an elderly couple walked past them and entered the restaurant.

In no time they finished their salads and were lingering over dessert, staring out at the colorful boats anchored near the dock.

Jenna said, "I knew you'd like this place, Kelcy. Miriam and I never eat anywhere else when she comes to visit me up here."

Kelcy smiled. She was getting used to Jenna's conversations that were sometimes hard to follow. "Yes, it's very charming."

"Oh, I should explain that Miriam is my dear friend from school days. Her eldest sister's son runs a little art gallery up here in summer. I know you'll like that, too. And he's such a nice boy. Bennett is a bit flaky, shall we say, but Miriam always points out he takes after his father's side. She can be so witty at times. Well, we'll stop in there to say hello. It's just down the street. But I must warn you, he had quite a reputation with the ladies. Even Miriam and I find ourselves blushing at his silly compliments."

Kelcy made some swift calculations, concluding this boy they were discussing had to be well past forty. "I'm sure I will enjoy meeting him and especially looking through his shop."

Jenna beamed. "Oh, you will, dear. Hawk mentioned to me that you were somewhat of an artist, too. Such a talented girl you are. It's no wonder he finds you so interesting. When I went into his study to say goodnight, he was on the telephone, and I happened to overhear him mention your name and some art supplies. He was acting very odd, though, I must say, and hung up so abruptly after I came in. Really, I wasn't eavesdropping at all, and I didn't ask for any explanations, but he was insistent on telling me anyway. That you were an artist, I mean. Oh, well, who can understand young people these days? Hawk will be twenty-eight in December, and I swear sometimes I think he's going on sixty!"

It was difficult to think clearly after having heard Jenna's revelation. Why had he been discussing her over the phone? "Jenna," Kelcy asked nonchalantly, "you wouldn't happen to know whom he was talking to?"

"I'm afraid not, dear, but I suspect it could have been someone at the main office. I hope not Mrs. Cranden, though. She might get huffy knowing how easily she can be replaced." Jenna smiled to herself.

Kelcy, however, was not smiling. There was only one other person she could think of to whom he could have been talking—his lawyer! But why would Hawk call him? Maybe he hadn't. Maybe the lawyer had called him to check up on her. That seemed very plausible.

Then Jenna was speaking again and Kelcy had to brush those thoughts aside.

"When we leave here, we'll go looking for a new pair of shoes for you. Hawk told me about that crazy dog chewing up your sandal."

And that was exactly what they did. Kelcy followed Jenna into a small boutique that carried everything from sport clothes to evening wear. She gasped at the price of a simple pair of jogging shoes, which the clerk quickly explained was the top of the line.

"I don't really think I need the top of the line, Jenna," Kelcy whispered.

"Of course you do, and we'll also try on those black dress shoes over there."

"Those are lovely," Kelcy exclaimed. "But, Jenna, don't you think that heel is a little too high and thin for you."

"Not for me, dear, for you. An old lady like me can't wear those, but they're perfect for you. And she'll try on that frilly white blouse with the dark-blue suit, too, please," Jenna told the clerk.

Kelcy rubbed her forehead. "Jenna, I can't afford those things," she said nervously.

"Oh, now don't talk silly. Hawk pays you a good salary, I'm sure. These are investments, dear."

Dizzy after reading the price tags, Kelcy treated the articles of clothing like gold as she went into the dressing room at the two women's insistence. Kelcy came out looking lovely in the classic outfit.

"And you won't even need alterations," the saleslady told her.

"Perfect," Jenna said as if that was suddenly the only word she knew. "And I'll have that blue sweater, that scarf in yellow and this gold chain, and, Kelcy, while you're changing, I think I'll try on a pair of those jogging shoes, too!"

If Jenna was always that extravagant, Kelcy thought as she came back out dressed in her own jeans and shirt, I'll have to remember to steer her away from such shops in the future.

Jenna was at the checkout counter talking to the clerk.

The saleslady took the outfit from Kelcy and began folding it for a box.

Kelcy smiled apologetically. "I'm sorry, but I really can't afford these. Just the jogging shoes, please." She took out her checkbook.

Jenna frowned. "Hawk insisted those shoes go on his account, young lady, and I won't hear of it any other way. Now, as for the other items, don't you like them?"

"I do, yes, but—"

"Well, no buts then. I'll charge them along with my purchases, and you can pay me when you can. All right, it's settled. While I finish here, you can drive the car up, so we don't have to carry all this."

"Jenna, I'm not sure I can pay—"

"Enough said now, Kelcy. Run along." Jenna turned back to the clerk and began talking again.

There was no use in further argument, Kelcy knew, so she went outside.

Once they were both in the car, driving away from the store, Jenna pointed to a small brick building on the other side of the street.

It was Miriam's nephew's place, she told Kelcy. "Let's drive to the parking lot at the front and stop."

Dismally, Kelcy wondered if Jenna bought art the way she bought clothing.

The gallery was a neat split-level jumble of displays. There were paintings, sketches, ceramics, wooden items, jewelry, weavings, various sculptures, and other things.

Kelcy smiled as a man in his middle twenties came down a short flight of steps and greeted them cheerfully.

"Good day to you, ladies. Is there something I can help you with?"

Jenna answered. "Yes, there certainly is!"

Kelcy watched her eyeing the jewelry case and wondered if perhaps she could get her out of the place before she bought out the whole collection. But jewelry didn't seem to be uppermost in her mind just then.

"This is still Bennett Sherman's gallery, isn't it?" she asked.

"Yes, it is."

"Is he here today? I'd like to say hello to him. I'm an old friend of the family. My name is Jenna Dole."

The young man looked a bit put out. "I'm sorry

to disappoint you, but Bennett won't be coming up until early September, just before we close. He's decided to teach summer classes at a Midwest university, and he left me in charge of the gallery. My name is Nat Collins. Would you care to look at the paintings over there?"

"Well, yes, we would." Jenna smiled. "I'm sorry to miss Bennett, of course. But his place is so unique, it always intrigues me."

As they reached the area of framed paintings, Jenna stopped and pointed to a barn scene. "Who is the artist of that one? I must know!"

"Why, I am!" the young man said.

Jenna put her hand to her throat. "What luck! Do you do commission work, Mr. Collins? Let me tell you why I ask. My nephew owns this old mill up here, about a twenty-minute drive. I'd love you to paint it just as you captured that barn on canvas. Could you do it?"

Nat Collins stared thoughtfully into space. "I might be able to come out and take a look. And if it inspires me, perhaps I could find time after gallery hours and on weekends."

"Price is no object," Jenna said.

Kelcy sighed deeply at the woman's generosity. Nat Collins appeared to be a talented artist, but so were a lot of others. She herself could easily have painted that barn scene just as well. Any second-year student might have.

"So what do you say?" Jenna asked.

"I'll do it, Mrs. Dole."

Kelcy could keep silent no longer. "Mr. Collins, I believe you should agree on a price up-front. I've had some experience, holding an art degree myself, and that is the general way commissions are done."

"Rightly so," he answered smoothly. "Shall we say the cost of materials plus eight hundred, then?"

Jenna looked pleased.

Kelcy was not. "Shall we say the cost of the materials and five hundred if, on completion, she likes it?"

Nat shook his head slowly. "You do drive a hard bargain, but since she's a family friend, I'll do it."

"Oh, wonderful! Now, just one more thing," Jenna smiled brilliantly. "I want this to be a surprise. We can't let Hawk see you out there with paint and canvas, can we? So how shall we do this?"

"I could do some of the work from a photograph after my initial sketches," Nat suggested.

"That would be good although you still must come to the mill for preliminary sketching. So how about this? You could masquerade as a fence painter by day. There's an old fence running adjacent to the bridge."

Nat nodded. "Excellent, Mrs. Dole. An assistant can take over for me here at the gallery for a while. And with daylight growing longer, after the gallery closes, I'll come out evenings to speed things up."

"And Kelcy can keep your sketches in her room with your paints, too, if that would be all right with both of you. Then you wouldn't be constantly dragging everything back and forth. And I always like to see a work in progress. That's important to me. Oh, but wait, that might make Hawk suspicious unless . . . Oh, this is perfect! I'll link the two of you romantically. Neither of you would mind the small deception, would you?"

Nat Collins said that he wouldn't mind in the least; Kelcy didn't say anything. She didn't like the idea at all. There had been enough deception with Hawk already. But how could she tell Jenna that without giving away Glen's secret? Life was becoming very complicated for her.

"Kelcy, you wouldn't mind, dear, would you?" Jenna persisted.

She sighed deeply. "I guess it would be all right. But Mr. Westbrook might not like the idea of my bringing friends to the house. After all, I am just an employee. What do we do if he objects to Nat's coming?"

"Oh, he won't say anything. Why should he care what you do with your free time, Kelcy?" Jenna laughed. "And if he gets bearish, I'll handle him. Then it's all set. We'll look forward to seeing you, Nat, in a few days."

They were back in the car and Jenna had just fastened her seat belt.

Kelcy asked, "Would you like to go anywhere else, or shall we start back to the house?"

Jenna seemed distracted, staring down the street. "What, Kelcy? Oh, nowhere else. Just drive home. That is so odd, you know. That dark-bearded man over there. I saw him in the restaurant, then again from the boutique-shop window when you went out to get the car, and just now he came out of Bennett's gallery. If I didn't know better, I would say he was following us. He did seem to be staring, too."

"Probably one of your admirers, Jenna," Kelcy laughed lightheartedly.

Jenna snorted. "Never, girl. He's way too young for me and much too old for you. Take a look. Do you know him?"

Kelcy glanced in the direction Jenna pointed. Indeed, there was a small, dark-bearded man with wavy black hair. But he quickly disappeared from sight. Something about the way he carried himself did seem familiar, yet that was the extent of it. Kelcy couldn't remember just then who walked like that. Probably hundreds of middle-aged men, she decided.

"I don't know anyone up here, Jenna." And suddenly all her attention was needed to maneuver through the increasing traffic. That mysterious stranger of Jenna's was pushed out of Kelcy's thoughts.

## CHAPTER EIGHT

Kelcy was busy typing letters a few mornings later when she heard footsteps behind her, and a voice said:

"Good morning, Kelcy—if I may be so bold as to call my new girlfriend that."

She glanced over her shoulder to see Nat Collins shuffling into the office.

"Nat! Why, hello! Aren't you working at the gallery today?"

He shook his head. "My assistant can handle things. It was such a nice day, I thought I'd make a start on that painting. So do I look the part of a starving fence painter?"

Kelcy laughed. He was dressed in white overalls, the kind house painters commonly wore, splashed with a dozen colors. An old hat worn backward covered his head.

"My, yes, you look extremely smart," she joked. "Tell me, did you take that getup into the backroom and dump paint on it, or are you the type who really gets his work all over himself?"

Net held his hand near his mouth and said in a mock whisper, "If you must know, I bought it in a thrift shop for half a buck. Some deal, eh?"

She easily agreed, and his light banter was amusing. But she could not help thinking if Hawk came in and saw her talking to Nat, he would not be amused.

Kelcy said, "Mr. Westbrook is out of his office right now. He usually goes out riding mornings when the weather is nice. But sometimes he doesn't. So maybe you'd better not make a habit of coming in here, just in case. He'd ask a lot of questions. And the less we have to tell him, the better."

Nat dramatically lifted an eyebrow. "Aha! Are you afraid of the old man?"

"No!" she snapped. "But he's not the most congenial person around. And he's not old either. He just gives that impression—very arrogant and—"

"A stuff-shirt snob, too good for the rest of us," Nat finished.

Kelcy sighed. "Close enough. Well, maybe I am a bit afraid of him."

The faintest grin spread over Nat's wide mouth. "Don't worry about it. The old lady told me he was out when I stopped by at that mansion. She also fixed things with the groundkeeper so everyone's story will be the same. It shouldn't take me long to crank out something that will please her. It's obvious she doesn't know beans about art."

For a moment Kelcy's stare grew cold. "What if I told her you said those things, Nat?"

He smiled at her innocently. "You won't. And you know for a fact that everything I said is true. Bennett Sherman clears a six-figure income from wealthy old gals just like her."

"Maybe so, but I won't stand by and let you defraud her, Nat."

"I know that, Kelcy. I have no intention of cheating her. Believe it or not, I'm a darned good artist when I apply myself. I took on this job as a sort of challenge to myself, something I haven't had for a long time. Now what about you?" Nat looked around thoughtfully. "This sure is some setup, a good subject to paint, a nice place to visit. But as the saying goes, I wouldn't want to work here. Why do you do it?"

"It's a long story, Nat. Maybe it's best if we both get on with our work!"

"Okay, I just stopped in to see a pretty smiling face," he said sardonically. "So then how do we pull this off if old Westbrook sees us together? Do I take you in my arms and smother you with kisses?"

"I don't think that's necessary, Nat!"

"Okay, okay, just teasing you, Kelcy. But we should do something friendly. How about a movie some night?"

That idea sounded harmless enough to Kelcy. However, with Hawk's house-arrest rules, she did not know if it would be possible to go.

All the same, she said, "Maybe, to the movie. We'll see."

"Right, I'll give you a call." He tipped his hat

and pulled out a small sketch pad from inside. "Now how's this for cloak-and-dagger stuff? He'll never know what I'm doing."

Kelcy laughed. She was feeling friendlier toward Nat already. "You've covered everything. Just don't forget to dab some paint on that fence occasionally."

"I won't. Oh, by the way, I left some paint and canvas with dear Mrs. Dole. She said she'd stash them in your room." Nat put his pad back under his hat.

Next he picked up a pencil from the holder on Kelcy's desk, his hand resting lightly on her shoulder. And at that moment Hawk Westbrook walked in.

He nodded to Nat, taken by surprise for only a second. Then his gray eyes rested on Kelcy. She had never seen him look so cold, so forbidding.

"You must be the new man Brad hired to paint the fence," Hawk said stiffly, speaking directly to Nat. "It's down by the bridge, parallel to the south road, where it's been for the past hundred years— not up here in my office."

"I know," Nat countered smoothly, "and a nice fence it is. A nice secretary you have here, too." Gallantly he bent down and brushed Kelcy's cheek with his lips. "See you later, honey." He left the office, whistling confidently.

Kelcy's face was a study in red from embarrassment. "We're just friends, that's all," she tried to explain quickly.

Hawk sighed in exasperation. "Perhaps I don't

give you enough work to occupy your time, Miss Kendal."

Enough work! Kelcy thought to herself. He had managed to supply her with tons of work, enough to satisfy ten secretaries. Her back, shoulders, fingers, and head ached from the typing she did each day. Her eyes blurred to the point where she wondered if perhaps she should be wearing glasses.

"What is it you want me to say, Mr. Westbrook? I have more than I can handle the way it is. Do you want me to come back after dinner and work a second shift?"

"I'll give that some thought," he said flatly, handing her a handwritten letter. "In the meantime, I want the file on the Biggs Company, names and addresses of all their stockholders, and this letter sent out to each one, offering them the present market price for their holdings. Get on it right after lunch!"

Kelcy glanced at the horseshoe paperweight on her desk and wanted to fling it at his broad back.

Hawk Westbrook had been working quietly for most of the afternoon, taking a few phone calls, reading through pages of reports, making notes here and there, completely oblivious to Kelcy's presence. She was thankful for that at least. It had been peaceful. But now she had to take a stack of letters in for his signature, and she was dreading it.

She shyly went up to the corner of his desk and put down the letters. "These are ready to be signed whenever you wish to—"

"Sit down," he said.

Kelcy sat down in the chair alongside his desk. She guessed that he wanted her to wait until he had affixed his name to every last letter, since he had not even looked up at her but had continued to read the report in front of him.

Several minutes passed. Finally he finished the report and leaned back in his chair, muttering, "Enough of this drudgery." He stood up, lazily leafing through his correspondence she had just typed. Then he sat on the edge of his desk and looked down at Kelcy.

Her eyes met his inquiringly. "Is there something you want from me?" Poor choice of words, she realized too late.

"Some information," was his rueful reply. "It was rumored that you and Miles were romantically involved. Is that true?"

Kelcy gasped at his shocking question. "NO! Our relationship was strictly business!"

"Then you deny ever dating him—dinners, shows, and the like."

She grimaced. "Why should I deny it? There were dinners, yes, not dates in any sense of the word. We worked long hours, and sometimes we ate together. That's all. I heard those rumors, too, Mr. Westbrook. But they didn't surface until after he disappeared and the police needed a suspect to put in their files. I recall only one time we went to the theater together. His friend gave him free tickets, and he asked me as a bonus for some research I had done for him the weekend before. I wanted to see that play and would have gone alone anyway."

Hawk looked at her. "But you weren't romantically involved, you say."

She put her chin up defensively. "No, I was not! And even if I had been, I can't see that it's any of your business, Mr. Westbrook."

"No," he said moodily, "it isn't my business." He turned away and stared out the window at the bright warm day. "And you had nothing to do with embezzling those company funds?" he shot at her, glancing back to catch her eyes with his penetrating gaze.

Kelcy was getting sick and tired of his insinuations and decided to be flippant. "But, of course, I did. We planned the whole thing over candlelit dinners. And it went off like clockwork. That's why I'm presently at his side enjoying myself in South America! The party I attended that Friday night was just a kick. I wasn't really desperate to find a job. I could have lived indefinitely, perhaps a whole lifetime, on the hundred-odd dollars in my checking account. But you know, Mr. Westbrook, I wish I had known about his plans. Maybe then I could have stopped him from making a stupid mistake."

"My apologies," he said in a dry voice. He smiled now, but it was not a friendly smile. "And since you brought up that party, Miss Kendal, tell me who stole my car!"

She gave him a cool look. "I told you once, twice, a hundred times I didn't know his name." That wasn't exactly a lie. She didn't know it at the time. "He was just a man who offered me a ride home."

"And you go with anyone who comes along, is that it?"

Kelcy snapped, "It wasn't like that at all!"

"Then how was it exactly?"

"He—well, he was leaving, and I was sitting on the steps wishing my friend Sandra would come out so we could leave, too. Only, he wasn't in much of a hurry because he stopped to talk." She started fidgeting, remembering their conversation.

"Go on," Hawk prompted.

"We just talked. One thing led to another, and I told him I was looking for a job. He said he could help me, then offered to drive me home."

Hawk scowled. "So you believed him. Without knowing a thing about him, not even his name, you let him drive you home."

It sounded very foolish, dangerous even, now. But that, more or less, was exactly what she had done. "Well, he sounded sincere, honest, anyway." And he was your cousin, she wanted to add but didn't.

"Oh, honest! Above all, honest," Hawk said angrily. "I suppose my Mercedes helped you make up your mind, too."

"I didn't know a thing about your Mercedes until we walked to the car. I was desperate for a job, and he said he might help me. But I was not desperate enough to get into a stolen car, had I known it was!"

Hawk narrowed his eyes. "You want me to believe you're not the type who would do anything for advancement. What if that guy would have made a pass?"

"He didn't! I doubt if Gl—"—she caught herself

just in time, coughing suddenly to cover her near mention of Glen's name—"if that guy was as crude or as sleazy as you think. He seemed very proper, not at all the type."

"All men are that type, Miss Kendal, given the chance. You're certainly an attractive girl—a beauty by some men's standards. A foolhardly, unwary, thoughtlessly impulsive beauty, however, from what you've told me and what I've seen for myself. Luckily I'm not the kind to be taken in by a pretty face—not like my cousin Glen, so it would seem."

For a moment Kelcy was floored. Did he know Glen had stolen his car? Or was he just fishing?

"What's that supposed to mean, Mr. West-brook?"

"Figure it out for yourself," he shot back. "You know, I should just let you get involved with that slick-talking Collins. It might teach you a lesson, but your education is not my business. So keep your distance from Collins. That's an order!"

Kelcy stood up. "An order I don't have to follow! You're not my guardian, and you can't choose my friends!"

"Normally, you would be right. But under the circumstances, and considering the large amount of money you owe me, you'd be wise to do as I say." A wicked smile creased the corners of his mouth. "How long do you think he'll be painting my fences if you don't?"

Kelcy shrugged helplessly. "All right! All right! I heard you." She wondered how Jenna would take the news. "Is there anything else, any more orders you'd like to issue, sir?"

"None at the moment, Miss Kendal."

"Very well. Then am I dismissed? I'd like to get back to my typing. As soon as you sign those letters, I can send them out."

Clearly unconcerned, he picked up a letter and read through it. "By the way, these will all have to be done over. I've decided to offer these stockholders market value plus ten percent to encourage them to sell. I want full control before I settle the deal."

Kelcy felt the color drain from her face. "Any more changes?" she asked as she picked up the pile of letters.

He looked at her sardonically. "What's the matter? Do you have a problem with that?"

"I—no."

She shook her head slowly, thinking. Not with the letters—with you, Mr. Charles Hawken Westbrook!

Head high, she walked back to her desk and sat down. She'd wanted to keep walking straight out the door, pack her things, and disappear, never to see him again. But that was impossible. She had promised Glen she would stay here three weeks, and here she would stay if it killed her.

# CHAPTER NINE

After work Kelcy sat alone at the round oak table in the kitchen, just as she had done each night since her arrival. Mrs. Meinert's meals were always delicious. Around six o'clock, having said good night to the cheerful cook as she left for the evening, Kelcy stacked her dishes in the dishwasher and went to her room.

She was tired, but it was too early for her to go to sleep, so she changed her clothes and decided to catch up on her ironing. A heaping pile of fresh laundry spilled over her basket in the corner. Beside it, Nat's art materials were scattered about. She gathered them up and put them in the closet next to her own art supplies. Then she took out the iron and board, set them up, and began her task. Kelcy hummed quietly to herself, working steadily until

105

she was finished. Just then there was a light rap on her door.

Kelcy called, "Come in," and Jenna hurried into the room.

"The phone, Kelcy. Someone is calling you. Please take it in the study, would you, dear?"

Befuddled, Kelcy tried to think. Who could possibly be calling her here? She glanced at Jenna. The kind woman was dressed in a smart linen suit with pearls circling her neck. It looked as if she might be going out.

"You look very nice, Jenna," Kelcy remarked.

"Thank you, dear. I'm just going to a card party in Sturgeon Bay with friends. In fact, they'll be here to collect me any second, so I must run. Don't forget the phone! Come now, follow me, in case you don't remember where the study is." Kelcy went along with Jenna. "In there, dear. The phone is on the desk. We really should have more extensions in this house. You can tell that to Hawk when you see him. Oh! There's my ride," she added, hearing the doorbell chime.

Now when would I see him? Kelcy wondered after Jenna had gone. But she didn't have long to wait, for no sooner had she entered the study than she saw Hawk sitting at the desk. He was filling out some type of form. She felt uncomfortable as she walked the rest of the way to the phone.

He was dressed in the same casual style that she was—old, faded jeans and a cotton shirt. He gestured to the receiver off the hook. If Nat Collins was on the other end, she thought nervously, she didn't know what she would say.

Kelcy picked up the phone. "Hello."

"Kelcy? Is that you? I can hardly hear you," a familiar feminine voice responded clearly.

"Oh, Sandra!" Kelcy sighed happily. "It's you! How did you get this private number?"

She heard Sandra laugh. "Well, it sure wasn't easy. I had to call Westbrook Industries, go through all kinds of foolishness. And believe me, the lady I finally ended up with sure didn't want to give it out. How are you?"

"Fine. Is anything wrong that you're calling?"

"Of course not. Why are you so negative, Kelcy? I just wanted to tell you that girl, Lucy Parker, sublet your apartment for now. She's still looking for a place of her own. How's your job?"

"My job? Well, I'm kept real busy." She glanced at Hawk.

He didn't seem to be listening. At least he hadn't reacted. He was still filling in that form.

"Is it nice up there?" Sandra asked.

"Lovely. The house is just beautiful!"

Sandra said, "Good. You needed a change of scenery. Lucy wants to know if she should send you a check or a money order for her share of the June rent. On the first, she'll just send it directly to the landlord. And you two can sort out the difference when she leaves or you come back or whatever."

Kelcy quickly said that a check would be fine and asked Sandra how things were going with her in the city. By the time Sandra had filled her in on all the latest news, including a detailed description of the new guy she was dating, Kelcy felt her spirits rise.

"So then, that's about it for me," Sandra was finishing. "I miss you, Kelcy. When do you think you'll get back?"

"Sooner than you think, maybe. So don't let Lucy get too settled in," Kelcy replied without thinking.

"Well, I'll tell her. Oh, by the way, she did say something that might interest you. She said the first night she moved in, some older guy came around looking for you. He really seemed shocked, then almost angry, that you had gone away. Poor Lucy! He pushed his way in and was asking her all kinds of questions. Did you have a new job? When were you coming back? And on and on. She was sure glad her brother was there at the time, helping her get settled in. He's like six feet and plays college football. That snoopy guy didn't give his name or anything or even say if he was a relative."

Kelcy shrugged. "Really? Maybe it was one of those nosy detectives still looking for clues on the Miles case."

"Who knows? She didn't tell him much, but your next-door neighbor happened to be in the hall and spilled all she knew. What an old gossip. You shouldn't tell her so much, you know. Anyway, he could have just been a salesman. I don't think it's anything to worry about."

"Probably not," Kelcy agreed, but she felt strange just the same. "Lucy didn't happen to say what that guy looked like, did she?"

Sandra sighed. "Well, I don't recall. Oh, yeah, come to think of it, she said he wasn't too tall, had black, black hair, like it could have been dyed, and he needed a shave. He gave her the creeps! Doesn't sound like anyone you'd be likely to know, does it?"

"No!" Kelcy agreed readily "It sure doesn't!"

"Okay, I'm going to hang up then and wash my hair. Keep in touch."

After they said their good-byes, Kelcy stood there for a moment, deep in thought, oblivious to her surroundings. What on earth could some strange man want with her? she wondered. Black hair, needing a shave. That almost fit the description of the man Jenna had drawn her attention to at Fish Creek. But, no, it couldn't be the same man. That thought was too ridiculous!

Hawk was suddenly standing beside her, touching her arm.

"Hey, what's the matter with you?" he asked. "You look pale as a ghost."

Her green eyes blinked, instantly focusing on the spot where his strong fingers made contact with the sleeve of her shirt. He turned her gently to face him. She trembled ever so slightly, and he noticed.

"So that was our infamous friend Sandra, was it?" He smiled.

"You were listening! Well, of course, you were."

"It would have been hard not to at that distance. I didn't hear you ask me to leave, after all."

"Because you wouldn't have gone if I had!"

Hawk smiled wryly. "Now that's something you'll never know, Miss Kendal. What did she want?"

Kelcy almost said it was none of his business.

"Nothing much—to say hi and to tell me a girl named Lucy Parker sublet my apartment."

"And that upset you?" Hawk asked.

"No, not that. Something that girl said about a man coming around wanting to see me." She really shouldn't have told Hawk Westbrook that, she knew, but strangely enough she felt better for confiding in him.

Hawk raised one eyebrow. "Perhaps you think it's the guy who stole my car coming around with some more larcenous ideas for you to help him with."

His suggestion was so preposterous Kelcy nearly laughed. However, she kept her amusement under control, smiling faintly. "No, I don't think that. I'm sure it's not him."

"How can you be sure of that?"

The suddenness of his question took her off guard. "Uh, well . . . it couldn't have been him because he didn't even know my name. And, besides, he didn't fit the description. This guy was older with a beard of sorts."

"Really?" Hawk asked derisively. "A beard upsets you so much that it makes you tremble."

"If you really must know," Kelcy sighed, pulling away from him, "what upsets me was the thing your aunt said. She noticed a man with a beard in Fish Creek. She thought it was just a coincidence that he happened to be everywhere we were—but now I'm not too sure."

Hawk shrugged. "Jenna always had a good imagination. She and her husband Egbert wrote mys-

teries years back when they lived in Scotland.
Don't put too much stock in what she says."

Kelcy was more than a bit put off by the way he
treated her news—almost as if she and Jenna were
dim-witted loonies.

"Well, good night, Mr. Westbrook," she said
curtly and turned to go.

He moved suddenly to stop her, glancing at his
watch as he did. "It's just seven-thirty. How about
taking a little walk with me down to the barns?
They shipped in a new mare today and I haven't
seen her yet. These are her registration papers.
Brad wanted to see them before I send them out. I
presume you like horses since Sue told me you can
ride. Or are you too worn-out from all the office
work I give you?"

His mouth was smiling, but his eyes weren't.
They were narrow and watchful. Kelcy nodded
shyly, her forehead creased in a puzzled frown.
Why in the world was he acting so pleasantly? He
must have some reason. But whatever it was, she
knew that if she did not accept his spur-of-the-mo-
ment invitation, he would never repeat it.

"I would very much like to see your horses, Mr.
Westbrook," Kelcy responded, carefully polite.

"Then shall we go?" he asked with unbelievable
courtesy.

Kelcy gazed at him with wide eyes. Hawk Westbrook was certainly an enigma.

Out on the front porch Guthrie lay sleeping.
Upon hearing footsteps, he jumped up, wagged his
tail, and headed toward his master.

"Hi, Guthrie!" Kelcy bent down to stroke the Doberman's back.

It was a lovely evening. The sun was setting, sending pinkish streaks across the pale sky. A gentle breeze stirred the shrubbery. Kelcy felt a sense of belonging with her surroundings, and she wondered if it would ever be possible to grow tired of this place.

As they walked toward the stables, followed by Guthrie, Hawk said, "You've got a way with dogs. In fact, you've got a way with almost everything, Miss Kendal."

"I expect that has a double meaning," she replied softly. He didn't answer. "Umm, I thought so."

"I suspect a smart girl like you can figure that out."

"And I guess I already have. You don't like me, Mr. Westbrook. You're only tolerating my presence here until I pay off the bill for fixing your car. You're doing your best to punish, insult, and humiliate me way above and beyond anything I deserve. Why I don't know. I didn't even steal your stupid car! And you can be abominably rude with very little effort!"

Everything seemed to stop, and Kelcy felt so drained she could have dropped to the ground. She hadn't meant to say the things she had. They'd just come pouring out.

There was a tall maple tree beside the path. Shakily she went to lean against it, desperately needing the support.

Neither of them spoke. Hawk had followed her every movement with his keen, perceptive eyes.

At last Kelcy said, "Okay, fire me if you must. Then try sending me off to jail. I just don't care anymore!"

Hawk looked at her curiously for a long moment. "Well, well!" He shook his head. "Toss a spark her way, and she can explode. Maybe Jenna's right. I am working you too damned hard."

He wasn't as angry as she thought he would be. In fact, he was merely mocking her more than anything else.

Kelcy took a deep, calming breath, and some of her strength returned. "You don't really need a secretary up here, Mr. Westbrook. With those modem computers, your city staff can handle everything as efficiently as I can, perhaps better . . . as if they were right at the mill. I can find some other way of paying that bill. Maybe Mr. Sawyer wasn't joking when he made me that job offer."

"I'll bet he wasn't," Hawk muttered under his breath. Then more loudly, in a no-nonsense tone, he said, "I need you. Now enough said! You're upsetting Guthrie." He smiled at that, glancing at the dog sitting nearby with ears alert, waiting for something to happen.

And something had happened. Something as unfathomable as any mystery. Something profound between her and this infuriating man. Hawk Westbrook had said he needed her! Of course, he could not have really meant that, she told herself quickly.

Kelcy suddenly turned away. "I'll go back to the house then."

"What for? You said you'd like to see the horses.

So you'll have to come to the stables. I'm not bringing them up to the house."

Silently she continued walking beside him, looking resolutely ahead.

As they neared the stables, Hawk ordered Guthrie to heel.

To Kelcy he explained, "I don't want him chasing the colts over in that field."

"Understandable," she said, her eyes fixed on five spindly-legged colts contentedly grazing near their mothers' sides.

Stopping for a moment, she ambled over to the fence and leaned along the top rail, careful to avoid touching the electric wire that ran parallel on the inside. Two identical chestnut foals with white-blanketed rumps caught her eye.

"Your Leopard mare has twins," she remarked brightly.

"Do you like Appaloosas?" he asked as he joined her.

She nodded. "The colorful blanket types especially."

"Those are the only ones we have now. The rest are quarter horses, thoroughbreds, and four nice Morgans. Anyway, those two foals are doing great."

Kelcy smiled. Just then one of the colts flopped down, rolled over, leaped up, and reared playfully. "Yes, I can see that," she laughed. "He'll be a handful."

"You think so? He's already halter broke. If he's too much trouble, we'll give him to you to train." Hawk's grin was infectious, and Kelcy couldn't stop the corners of her mouth from turning up into a smile.

"You think I couldn't?" she challenged light-heartedly.

"Is that what I just said?"

"You said—" She stopped.

At that moment Kelcy was so confused by his congenial mood, she couldn't recall exactly what he had said. But he had to be up to something. He just had to be.

"I heard you tell your friend over the phone that the place was beautiful. Does that mean you like it up here?" Hawk asked as he slowly bent down to pick up a sharp rock and toss it off to the side. Guthrie stood, eager to chase it. But one sharp word from his master, and he settled down.

Kelcy said, "It's lovely! Of course, I like it."

Hawk stared out over the vast green fields. "There is a sense of timelessness about everything around here. No hurry, no urgent rush to be any-where. It all seems to stay the same even though that's impossible. And the mill has a certain lure to it."

"Lure, yes, that is the perfect word." Kelcy smiled. "That's how I felt the first time I saw it. It has a certain effect."

Without warning, Hawk gently ran his hand down her cheek, laughing softly at the look of sur-prise registered on her pretty face. Brushing back a wisp of chestnut hair that had escaped the braid hanging down her back, he said, "Are you really just a decent, innocent girl with mistaken loyalties, Miss Kendal? True, I branded you as completely no good when I first saw you out cold in my car at the accident scene. Now I'm not so sure." His voice was strangely husky.

Kelcy could feel her pulse quicken, a sensation that was making her weak. She wanted to look at him, but she could not face him. Finally, she did. Amusement was in his eyes.

In the next moment, he caught Kelcy to him firmly, his mouth pressing down on hers, his demanding kisses finding an ardent response.

Guthrie chose that moment to bark, reminding them of his presence.

Hawk laughed softly as he tenderly eased her away. "I wonder if that meant approval or disapproval."

Kelcy hastily looked toward the stables, her lips still tingling. Now and then she had irrationally wondered what it would be like to be kissed by this man. At last she knew—disturbing, bewildering, and curiously stirring.

Forcing herself to face him, although it was most humbling, she said accusingly, "He's not the one you should be asking for approval. Why did you do that?"

"For the same reason you allowed me to. It was just a kiss, Kelcy. I wanted to know. . ." He did not finish his sentence. "Let's just say it was a revealing moment." He was grinning most infuriatingly.

Kelcy was tempted to slap his face. She raised a shaking hand, but then just brushed back some wispy hair.

The moment was revealing, he had said. Oh, yes, it had been that. She knew now that she could

hate this man intensely, yet still respond shame-
lessly to his kiss. She tried to forget the whole business.

The rest of the tour was pleasantly uncompli-
cated. Sue and Brad Gill greeted them in a cozy loft
office that had once been used for hay storage.

Before long, after Kelcy had admired Sue's collection of antique horse carvings, Brad enlisted
Hawk's help in some horseshoeing chores. Meanwhile, Sue gladly agreed to take over showing
Kelcy the stables. Fine, sleek horses poked their
velvety noses over half doors in the stalls. Now and
then Sue would take the time to catch one of the
show animals and bring it out into the breezeway
for Kelcy's inspection. Their last stop was at a
corner stall that contained the new mare.

Sue handed Kelcy a lead rope and opened the
sliding partition. "Go catch her, Kelcy. She's a real
Morgan beauty. A real friendly, people-loving
horse, I'm told. We bought her from an eighteen-
year-old girl who needed the money for college in
the fall."

Kelcy felt sympathetic. "Poor kid, I know how
that goes," she replied as she stroked the bay's
muzzle.

The mare certainly seemed to like her and, indeed, had the looks of a champion. Talking softly
to the affectionate animal, Kelcy snapped on the
lead and brought her out to the center of the barn.

Sue was busy shaking out a saddle blanket. "We
all know how that goes. Brad and I did our share of
sacrificing, too. But don't feel too sorry for the girl.

From what her mother said, she can always ride her sister's horse."

Hawk and Brad strode through the main door just then with tools still in their hands. They stopped to look at the mare.

"Saddle her up, Sue, and take her for a ride," her cheerful husband suggested. "We'll start her out slowly until she gets used to her surroundings."

"Let's let Kelcy ride her—I'll get my old faithful buckskin, Dusty, and we can take the short trail. It's still light enough yet."

Kelcy looked at Hawk, wondering what he would say to Sue's idea. Surprisingly enough, he didn't say anything. He just nodded.

Before she knew it, Kelcy was safely mounted and loping down a sandy trail with evergreens on one side, the river on the other, beside Sue on Dusty.

They stopped for a rest, allowing the horses to drink before walking them over a footbridge.

"What's this mare's name?" Kelcy suddenly asked.

Sue looked thoughtful. "I don't know that she has any formal one. She's just a number on a form until she's permanently registered. The previous owners didn't bother to file. They might have called her Star because of her white forehead mark —or was that their other horse? You name her!"

"No, I couldn't do that!" Kelcy laughed. "Mr. Westbrook should do that himself."

Sue flipped her reins gently against Dusty's shoulder to chase off a pesky fly. "Oh, he won't care. Besides, I thought I heard him tell Brad he got this horse for you to ride while you're working here." She swatted another bug. "We better be starting back. The mosquitoes are out, and it'll be dark soon."

In a mild state of confusion, Kelcy urged her mount into an easy canter, following Sue on Dusty back to the stables.

When the horses were cooled down and put away, Kelcy said goodnight to the Gills and walked through the barn to the main door. She stepped outside, starting for the path that led to the house. In the shadows from the yard light, with flashlight in hand, Hawk was leaning lazily against a decorative wagon in front of the stables. He seemed to be waiting for her.

"Enjoy your ride?" he asked.

She stopped when she saw him. "Yes, very much, thank you," she answered awkwardly.

He strode over to her. "Then I'll escort you back to the house. You never know what is lurking in these woods."

Kelcy looked around. "Where is Guthrie, anyway?" She hadn't meant that to be amusing, but it turned out that way—at least to Hawk.

He threw back his head and laughed. "I didn't mean Guthrie, that harmless good-natured pup. But where he is is anyone's guess. More than likely, up at the house. A few minutes ago, he was here, barking and growling, the hair on his back standing straight up. And then he tore down the path—I imagine in pursuit of a rabbit!"

She sighed and began walking briskly. She was tired. It had been a long day. All she wanted now was to get away from Hawk, to be by herself—to forget everything that she had heard and everything that had happened. With easy, long strides, he quickly caught up to her.

Away from the yard lights, Hawk used his flashlight to illuminate the path. They hurried along, slapping down night insects as they went. Neither spoke until they entered the kitchen. There Hawk asked her:

"Did you leave all these lights on?"

"No, I did not!" Kelcy answered him abruptly. "It was still light when I went to my room after dinner. There was no need for lights. Maybe one of the cleaning staff . . ."

"Well, maybe. Some nights the part-timers work late, but I was sure tonight they all left early." Hawk shrugged and flipped the switch that snapped them off. Now only the hallway was lit.

To Kelcy's irritation, he followed her to her bedroom door and waited there. Now what did he want? she wondered as her fingers touched the ornate knob. Kelcy didn't exactly know what to say, but she thought she should say something.

"Goodnight then, Mr. Westbrook. I enjoyed seeing the stables. If you don't mind, I'd just like to clean up in the shower and get some sleep."

Hawk raked his fingers impatiently through his dark hair; his perfect cut fell neatly into place. "Right. I was just about to say—since you haven't been on a horse in some time—you'd better make that a hot shower because in the morning you'll feel the stiffness. Get a good night's sleep. I won't expect to see you in the office until after ten." With that he moved off abruptly.

Kelcy shook her head. Honestly, that man! She just didn't understand him. Perhaps she never would. Sighing to herself, she opened the door and flicked the light switch. But the overhead fixture remained dark.

"Oh, darn, must be some burnt-out bulbs," she said out loud, annoyed because she had no idea where to find the replacements. Well, the light bulbs could wait till morning.

Familiar with the room arrangement, Kelcy confidently started for the bathroom where the dim night light cast a shadowy glow under the door.

Then she struck something with her foot and cried out in pain. By all her calculations, nothing should have been there. Just then she thought of the lamp on her nightstand. Groping her way to the small table, she fumbled in the darkness until her fingers found the lamp base.

When Kelcy turned on the light, she was stunned. Strewn all over the room was her once neatly folded laundry. The ironing board was tipped over, and Nat's art supplies—his paints, brushes, and sketch pads—lay everywhere. It looked as if a whirlwind had hit.

Who and why? She was angry now, wanting answers. The thought of burglary had never crossed her mind but vandalism had. Hawk Westbrook had done this! She spun around and headed for the door. Her fingers roughly grasped the knob. But as she twisted it sharply, she heard movement behind her and felt a strong clasp like a vise around her waist.

Another arm pressed against her throat, and something strange-smelling, something suffocating, covered her face.

She struggled wildly. She fought as she had never fought in her life and still she couldn't get free. The room was swaying. White sparks filled her head.

Kelcy screamed, but it was not easy. It took all her remaining strength. She tried to scream again. She didn't know if she had because the white sparks had exploded into blackness, into nothing.

## CHAPTER TEN

"Kelcy!" The sound of her name came from far away, and a heavy gray mist cleared into brightness.

Why was everyone staring at her? Kelcy wondered as she blinked open her eyes. She was lying on a strange bed, and Hawk Westbrook was watching her from a chair by the bedside. Next to him stood his Aunt Jenna and two people she did not recognize.

"Good, she's finally coming around," Hawk said to the others. Then he turned to her. "You're going to be fine. It was some sort of art substance that contained ether on that rag. You were overcome by the fumes." And he smiled.

Hawk Westbrook smiling? Kelcy's eyes widened as she tried to sit up.

"Kelcy, dear, what happened?" Jenna asked,

123

looking very worried. "Hawk thinks you surprised a burglar."

"A—a burglar?" Kelcy frowned, gently rubbing her forehead. Her thoughts were muzzy. "I'm not so sure. I don't have anything valuable worth stealing. Someone was in my room, though. After I found the light and saw the vandalism, I started for the door with the intention of finding Mr. Westbrook. At first I thought—well, it doesn't matter. I remember turning the knob, hearing a noise, then being grabbed from behind, and a rag was clamped over my face. I screamed, and then I must have blacked out." She looked around the comfortably furnished room. "Where are we?"

Jenna bent down and patted her hand. "Well, forget about that terrible fright for now. You're in the second-floor guest room. Hawk is in the next room, and I'm down the hall if you need anything. You couldn't possibly stay downstairs until the fumes clear and the girls clean it up."

"Have you thought of more security?" the short, pudgy man behind Jenna asked Hawk. "Since the summer onslaught of tourists, there seem to be a few undesirables in the area."

"More each year, it does seem," a thin, perky little woman spoke out. "Why, Ruth Hill told me the other day someone smashed their birdbath and broke their front window with a rock. You know, Jenna, she and her family live on the lakeshore in their lovely two-story summer home. And I believe last month someone spray-painted their neighbor's garage door. Oh, and then, too . . ."

The conversation went on to include every crime

that had been committed in the county over the past six months, none of which seemed to resemble what had happened here, however.

Suddenly Jenna said, "Oh, my, in all this confusion, I almost forgot to introduce my friends to you, Kelcy. This is Mr. and Mrs. Palmer—Ivan and Lydia. Miss Kendal is my nephew's secretary, although I already think of her as one of the family."

Kelcy smiled at all of them.

"My dear, Miss Kendal," Lydia said, "we were so shocked to hear what happened. Ivan and I had just brought Jenna home when we saw Hawk carrying you upstairs. Heavens! We didn't know what to think! Even this lovely old house isn't spared crime nowadays. It makes me wonder if we shouldn't call off our plans entirely."

Jenna shook her head. "No, no, Lydia, we won't let some old burglar put us off. Our idea is perfect. We'll get together and work out the details later."

"How odd," Ivan suddenly said, "that only one room was vandalized. And how fortunate! Some of your lovely antiques are priceless, Jenna. At least paints and clothing can easily be replaced."

Jenna shrugged and shivered. "You're so right, Ivan. And we can thank Kelcy for foiling that intruder's plan. He was surely going to check the whole house, but she surprised him."

Kelcy cleared her throat shyly. "I'm afraid I didn't do much, Jenna. And it was the other way around. He surprised me."

"You did fine, dear. The most important thing is that you weren't seriously harmed. They didn't find any clues or have any leads, did they, Hawk?"

Hawk paused, almost as if he was reluctant to answer. "Not yet, but the police have been notified. I wish I'd gotten a look at the guy. When I reached her room, he had already fled and was slamming the kitchen door. Then I saw Kelcy on the floor and was more worried about her than running down the burglar—if it was a burglar."

"Well, I should hope you were more worried about Kelcy," Jenna said sharply. "That is police business. If the intruder had been carrying a gun or other weapon—we won't even think about that! Kelcy, dear, can you give them a description?"

She heard Hawk's mocking laugh in the background, followed by a mumbled oath, and knew he had to be thinking of that night he and his lawyer had asked her to describe Glen. Ironically, her answer was much the same.

"I'm afraid not. He grabbed me from behind and pressed a cloth over my face, as I said before. Then I blacked out."

"You had time enough to scream," Hawk cut in. "I had just started up the stairs and I heard you. What else can you remember? The police want to question you in the morning."

The police again, Kelcy thought tiredly. She recalled the Miles investigation. She knew what sort of questions they would ask and tried to retrace her actions.

"The room was dark when I entered. I tried the light switch on the wall, and it didn't work."

"He knocked out some of the wires when he deactivated the alarm system. That we quickly discovered," Hawk informed her. "It almost looked like an inside job. He knew where everything was, and he also seemed to know we were all out."

"Not necessarily, Hawk," Jenna said with a pensive look. "He could have gotten our phone number from any number of sources and called—to find no answer. Our line here is separate from both the stables and the mill office. It's a common trick of burglars. We've had a lot of workmen up here in the past few months. Sometimes the crew boss will take on an extra man or two to make a deadline without checking too closely on their backgrounds."

"Which brings to mind that Collins fellow," Hawk added. "He seemed damned free around the mill. I'll have a word with Brad."

Jenna's eyes squinted fractionally. "That nice young man! Really, Hawk. He's Kelcy's friend. It couldn't be him. I met and talked to him while he was working. It just isn't possible."

"Miss Kendal has an unhealthy talent for making friends too easily," Hawk replied stiffly. "And she's way too trusting, as you are, Jenna. I can't see why we need a fence painter around here anyway. What's the matter with Brad's helpers?"

"You don't believe it could have been Mr. Collins, do you, Kelcy?" Jenna asked nervously.

"No, I don't," Kelcy replied.

"And how can you be so sure, Miss Kendal, since you didn't see your attacker?" Hawk flung back at her accusingly. "Perhaps he came to visit you, was angry that you were out, and decided to destroy your art things for spite."

Kelcy     laughed.     "That's     ridiculous!     He

wouldn't—" She caught herself in time. She had
been about to say Nat wouldn't destroy his own art
supplies, for none of her paints or brushes had been
touched. They were all safely packed and locked in
her suitcase on the floor of her closet, just where
she had put them the night of her arrival. She had
been too busy to unpack them. "He wouldn't do
such a thing. What would be his motive?"

"I just told you. Spite, jealousy."

"Jealousy?" Jenna responded with a raised voice.
"Now, Hawk, you go too far. Jealous of Kelcy! He
likes Kelcy. He told me that himself. Think of some
real suspects. And for heaven's sake, don't go telling that ridiculous theory to the police."

Kelcy said, "It really couldn't have been Nat
Collins, Mr. Westbrook. He's tall and thin. If he'd
grabbed me by the waist, he would have had to
bend down, making it impossible to put that rag
over my face from the angle the attacker did. Although I was panicky when I fought to get loose, I
now realize the intruder was my height or shorter
and solidly built."

Hawk leaned toward her, exasperated, his eyes
hard. "Well, you were the only one there. We only
have your word for it, don't we?"

"Kelcy's word is good enough for me," Jenna
said. She turned to the girl. "Perhaps we should all
leave since you're safe now and need your rest
more than anything. It must have been a very
frightening experience for you, Kelcy. Think pleasant thoughts, and tomorrow I have a real surprise
for you, something you'll enjoy."

"That is an excellent idea," Mrs. Palmer agreed.

"We must be leaving soon, anyway. Come, Ivan," she ordered lightly and held out her hand to the old, distinguished-looking man.

"Hawk, if you'll be so kind as to come along with us to the living room, the Palmers and I have something we'd like to discuss with you," Jenna said sweetly. "It won't take too long, and we'll need your approval."

He nodded, giving Kelcy one long, dark look before getting up from the chair. "Now, more than ever, you had better take that hot shower, Miss Kendal. You even have paint smudges in your hair."

"I think you're right, Mr. Westbrook. I'll just go back down—"

"You stay right here in this room and use the bath through that door. It's fully equipped with towels and soap, and Jenna brought up your nightgown. I don't want you touching anything in your room until the police finish their investigation." With that he turned and followed the others, stopping just long enough to say, "Kelcy, you certainly do attract trouble!" Then he closed the door.

Later, as she lay in bed, Kelcy heard movement in the next room. Jenna had said it was Hawk's room. She felt safe knowing he would be sleeping just beyond that wall. She felt strangely comforted, too. Earlier, she had been annoyed by his suspicions of Nat Collins. As a motive for vandalism, Hawk had accused Nat of jealousy. Kelcy smiled to herself. She surely didn't want Nat's jealousy. If any one was to be jealous, she wanted it to be Hawk.

Hawk jealous? Now why should she want that? she asked herself.

But she knew why. She remembered how she had enjoyed that kiss.

Don't be stupid, Kelcy told herself severely, punching her pillow. She couldn't imagine what had come over her. In a short time she'd be leaving this house, never to set eyes on Charles Hawken Westbrook again.

Go to sleep, said a small voice in the back of her mind. And have pleasant dreams. But for some reason, sleep eluded her for quite a long time.

The next day Kelcy did not go up to the mill to work. She spent the morning going through her things with the police investigators to see if anything had been stolen. Despite the mess the intruder had made, robbery did not appear to be his motive. She found nothing missing. But then, of course, as she had informed the police and everyone else, she had nothing of real value.

Her interview with the two police officers—one burly middle-aged man and his partner, a cheerful younger woman—was not the strain that Kelcy had anticipated. These two were more friendly and helpful than the detectives who had questioned her about the Miles case. They filled out their report as thoroughly and courteously as was possible, dusted for fingerprints, which proved to be a waste of time, for it appeared the intruder had worn gloves, and thanked Kelcy for her cooperation. They added that they would be assigning an extra patrol car to watch the area for the next week. They were out by noon.

After lunch, Sue Gill sent in one of her part-time college girls to help with the cleanup. Kelcy, however, preferred to do most of the work herself, carefully scrubbing Nat's paints from everywhere on the polished wood floor. Luckily no paint had touched the braided rugs or the lovely quilt, she thought as she put away her rags and admired the room. Everything was back in order at dinnertime.

When the meal was over, Jenna came in to see Kelcy, who was in the process of making up a list of replacement supplies for Nat. Hawk's aunt brought a small red folder with her.

"My dear," she began, "you've done an excellent job with the room. No one would ever know it had been vandalized. Sorry I couldn't be here to help you, but I had important business with the Palmers, which is the main reason I stopped by."

Kelcy smiled at her and thanked her for her concern, adding that she really hadn't expected Jenna to do any scrubbing on hands and knees.

Jenna thoughtfully looked around. "I don't like to admit it, but I think you're right. At seventy-four, those days are behind me. Ah, but forget that! Remember last night I told you I'd have a pleasant surprise. Well, wait till you hear. Let's go into the kitchen where I can spread out my materials."

With growing curiosity, Kelcy shrugged and followed her silently down the hall to the kitchen. There Jenna pulled out a chair and sat down behind the oak table, busily taking papers from her folder and spreading them out in a semicircle. Looking over the dear lady's shoulder, Kelcy eyed several sketches and one diagram.

"Well, what do you think?" Jenna asked enthusiastically.

"I think this one in the center looks like a rough map of sorts and the others look like sketches. That's the mill—very nice!"

"Oh, Kelcy!" Jenna burst into delighted laughter. "I've been so busy trying to get your thoughts on the matter that I've forgotten to tell you what's up. Old age muddles the mind, you know, dear."

Kelcy wore a puzzled expression on her face as she sank down in the chair beside Jenna's. "Well, are you going to tell me, or must I guess?" she asked playfully.

"Oh, yes, of course!" Jenna chuckled. "In the spirit of Fourth of July celebrations, which will be in approximately two and a half weeks. Let's see, today is the seventeenth of June—isn't that correct?"

"Correct," Kelcy agreed. She had been keeping close track on the days, counting them down, since she had started working for Hawk on the tenth. Today she had been there exactly one week. There were two more to go until July first, when Glen had promised he would confess to Hawk and clear her name. She was waiting anxiously for that day to come.

"Kelcy, are you listening? You look so far away."

"Yes, Jenna. Oh, I'm sorry, I was thinking about the date. Yes, it's the seventeenth. Now what were you saying about the Fourth?"

Jenna took a deep breath. "Well, not the Fourth because of all the parades and fireworks. But the fifth of July. Many people are on vacation, and it starts off the summer fun. We—Lydia, Ivan and a few members of our historical group, including myself—are planning a tour of homes on that day. Five authentic houses from the last century will be featured in this area. The public shall be invited to view our open houses from nine A.M. to five P.M. Our mill, and the house and grounds, will be the highlight. We'll decorate for the occasion. Also we thought we would set up an arts-and-crafts fair down by the mill featuring some local artists. Already there is a positive response from the artists we contacted today. And Nat Collins gave us a list of people to call. How does that sound?"

"Great, but can you put this all together on such short notice?" Kelcy asked.

"With a lot of help. Hawk had some doubts about the idea because of last night's break-in, but the local police have given their support. I was hoping you'd help us, Kelcy. You could give tours and such in costume."

Kelcy was speechless. Under any other circumstances, she would have loved to be part of such an event. But to agree would be letting Mrs. Dole down, since she was planning to leave several days before this tour would take place. But what reason could she give Jenna now for refusing?

"I can help with the arrangements on my free time, but my office job must come first, Jenna. Your nephew has a lot of work. And about giving tours, perhaps Sue or one of her staff could do them. I'm afraid I'd be too shy for that type of thing."

"Oh, that's silly, Kelcy. Once you start. you'll be fine. But that's a marvelous idea about Sue and the girls. There will be places for all of them. And Hawk will give you the time off. I'll insist he free you from those dreary secretarial duties to help us. He won't much care for the idea, I suspect, but he's outnumbered."

Swallowing hard, Kelcy nervously looked over the papers before her. If Jenna insisted, she would just go along with the plans for now. Later she would make arrangements for one of the other girls to fill in. "Is it just these five homes and the mill I'll have to worry about?"

"Oh, each owner has taken responsibility for their own property. You and I shall just concentrate on the house and mill. There'll be advance ticket sales and maps to be printed and such. But we already have help lined up for that. One of our members just happens to own a newspaper. Now wait till you hear this!" Jenna clapped her hands happily. "I've saved the best for last. The perfect ending to the open-house tour."

Kelcy looked at Jenna suspiciously. Every time she used the word "perfect," her mind was set like granite. And what followed usually meant something lavish, impractical, and almost certainly tremendously expensive. "What would that be, Jenna?"

"A charity ball, historical in theme and reminiscent of those bygone years, held in our very own third-floor ballroom. It's such a lovely setting."

When Kelcy heard this, her mouth fell open. "Jenna, those types of things are usually planned months in advance. The room would have to be papered, the floor possibly refinished or protected. There would have to be musicians hired, refreshments. And Hawk, what does he say to this? From what I know of him, he likes his privacy. virtual strangers would be tramping through his home."

"Oh, Kelcy, you do worry so! Naturally Hawk said no initially, but he finally agreed. Actually the third floor is in excellent shape. All it needs is a good airing and a cleaning. I've arranged for a cleaning firm to begin work the day after tomorrow. The main house will be roped off for the evening, so only the stairway and gardens shall be open for public use then. I thought you would be as excited as I am. Why the frown?"

"I am excited, Jenna, but is it practical?"

"We shall see, I expect. We'll start work tomorrow early." Jenna gathered up her papers and carefully placed them in her red folder.

Kelcy leaned back and sighed. "Then I suppose I should go down to the mill office tonight and finish typing some letters Mr. Westbrook wanted done."

"Oh, nonsense! Let Mrs. Cranden and her crew do some work for a change. I bet she's taking long lunches and more coffee breaks than she's ever taken in her life for want of something to do. And, besides, Hawk drove down to his city office early this afternoon. He'll be gone overnight. There's a party he wanted to attend tonight, and he said not to expect him back until late tomorrow evening. That reminds me. Taking advantage of his absence, I've invited Nat Collins to come out to sketch tomorrow."

"Which reminds me," Kelcy said moodily, feeling put out that Hawk had not told her of his plans, "I'll have to replace his art supplies. I was making a list—"

"Yes," Jenna absently broke in. "Why would anyone want to destroy them in such a fashion? It's beyond me."

It was beyond Kelcy, too. Just then, as she stood up, Guthrie's bark came from outside the kitchen door. She walked over to let him in. The sleek, mischievous dog ambled over the glossy tiles, carrying something in his mouth.

"He's got something, Jenna," Kelcy said as he playfully stood before her, growling ridiculously.

Used to his antics, Jenna reached down and tugged a piece of cloth from his mouth. "Where do you suppose he got this?" she asked, turning it over in her hand. "It looks like part of a jacket pocket from one of those denim vests some of the artists wear up here. Bennett Sherman sells them in his gallery. I know because I thought of buying one myself the other day when we were in there. The pocket would be a great place to put my things when I go on nature walks with my birdwatching club."

Kelcy came over and examined the cloth closely. "It sure does look like that, Jenna. And Bennett's gallery isn't the only place they sell them. I saw them in several shops that day, and the price was much lower," she added for good measure. "But where would Guthrie get such a thing?"

"Where, indeed?" Jenna sounded mysterious. "You don't suppose our Guthrie had a run-in with the burglar, do you?"

Kelcy shook her head. "I don't know, Jenna, but he was no burglar. That was proven. Remember, he didn't take anything."

"That's right, he didn't. However"—she held up a finger—"he sure seemed to have a fascination for your paints."

"Nat's paints," Kelcy corrected. "Are you thinking the intruder was just a frustrated artist doing his thing?" she laughed softly.

Jenna chuckled. "I'm not sure what I'm thinking. As a matter of fact, I'm too tired to think. Let's just forget we ever saw this and put that whole incident out of our minds. Tomorrow we have plans to make for the upcoming festivities."

"Perhaps we should forget this," Kelcy whispered softly. She patted Guthrie on the head while watching Jenna get out of her chair and tuck her folder under her arm. The cloth, she noticed, peeked over its edges. Now what would Jenna do with that chewed-up thing? she wondered.

Just then Jenna said, "Since Hawk won't be here tonight, why don't you keep Guthrie in your room? He's not the best of guard dogs, but he's better than nothing. And he'll sleep quietly on the rug in front of the fireplace, I think. At least he does when he's in my room."

Kelcy agreed to keep the dog, said goodnight to Jenna, and promised she would lock the kitchen door and activate the alarm—which had been repaired—before going to bed.

It was hours later, after she had taken Guthrie for a long evening romp, that Kelcy sat on the side of her bed and slipped off her shoes. She was about to crawl under the covers and turn off the light when she looked over at Guthrie to see the Doberman stretched out on the rug in front of the fireplace, growling softly in his sleep.

Just where Jenna said he would sleep, Kelcy thought, smiling to herself. Jenna was usually right about everything. But had she been right in suggesting that they forget the piece of torn pocket the dog had brought in?

Kelcy shrugged. Perhaps it meant nothing. So why did it keep nagging at the back of her mind? Why?

"Oh, Guthrie, if only you could talk," she whispered softly and reached for the light switch. But now she found that she was too restless to sleep. So she turned on the light again, picked up the book on the nightstand—the one Hawk had brought her—and began reading.

After looking at the first few pages of general history, she leafed through to the part describing Hawk's Mill as it had been over a hundred years before. Hawk's Mill it had been called even then. Charles Hawken Westbrook had not been handing her a line when he had told her how it had been named. Kelcy snapped the book shut and punched her pillows resentfully. Damn that man! Did he always have to creep into her mind?

It was a sure bet he wasn't wasting any of his thoughts on her, Kelcy guessed. He hadn't even had the courtesy to inform her that he would be gone for a day or so. That in itself told her how little he cared. By now he was enjoying himself at his fancy city party in the company of some lucky woman—and not just any woman. She would be a beautiful and witty date, Kelcy imagined.

And why can't you stop thinking about him, Kelcy Kendal? an inner voice taunted her. You mustn't. It's hopeless. Think about something else!

"Two more weeks," she whispered to herself. Her eyelids drooped and she put down the book, then switched off the lamp. "Two more weeks, Hawk, and I shall escape you," she murmured before sleep claimed her.

## CHAPTER ELEVEN

Hawk's Mill lay dreaming beneath the cloudless azure sky as Kelcy carefully dabbed some opaque stain across the split-rail cedar fence. The sounds of summer drifted through the woods with the warm breeze. Bees droned in the pollen-filled fruit trees of the distant orchard, while under the bridge colorful ducks swam in the clear water. In spite of her desire to get away, she knew she would miss it.

Kelcy put down her brush and sighed when she saw that the bucket was nearly empty. She had dressed for comfort, wearing bright red shorts and a paint-splattered, oversized shirt that had once been white. She had long ago kicked off her jogging shoes and was thoroughly enjoying the fine day.

Behind her, several yards away, Nat Collins sat on his folding stool with canvas in front of him. He was concentrating on his painting.

"You know, Nat," Kelcy called to him, "the way this old fence is soaking up the stain, we'll need at least two more five-gallon pails."

Nat laughed. "Truthfully, my dear, I don't care. It wasn't my idea to paint that fence. Although it looks nice, that fresh stain is covering a hundred years of charm."

"It might just be that it's preserving it for a hundred more," she said. "How are you coming along?"

He grinned. "Get up and come see for yourself. You better stop that fence staining, anyway. If you finish the darned thing before I do this painting, what excuse will I have for coming up here?"

"Oh! We couldn't have that," she laughed scoffingly as she dropped the lid on the bucket to keep what little stain she had left from drying out and got to her feet, heading his way.

Standing behind him, she studied Nat's work thoughtfully. She had to admit that the man had talent, yet still she decided to make a suggestion. The corner where the ducks gathered was possibly too dark. She thought the sun softened it more than he had and she discreetly told him so.

Nat sighed deeply and held up his hand. "Critics, critics—alas, I was just thinking that myself."

Kelcy laughed and sat down on a patch of grass beside him. The better she got to know him, the more she found herself liking him. Her first harsh opinion had softened considerably as she realized Nat could be good company, pleasant, cheerful— even sensitive. With a serious interest in his artwork, she reached for a tube of yellow oxide and handed it to him.

"Why don't you try adding a touch of this? It might lighten that green to just the right intensity," she suggested.

Nat opened the tube with interest, dabbed a spot of paint on his palette, mixing until he had the desired effect. "These paints of yours are great, Kelcy. I sure wish you'd change your mind and sell me your kit. Will you?"

She shook her head. Nat had asked her that same question yesterday when she had first brought it out for him to use. She thought it only fair that she should supply temporary replacements for the paints he'd lost as a result of the break-in. "Sorry, Nat. Like I said before, after you made your first overly generous offer, I plan to keep them."

"Well, maybe you'll come around if I up my offer."

"Your offer was high enough, if I had wanted to sell, but I don't."

"Name your price. That case is so unusual, so unique. I'd really love to have it." Nat eyed it admiringly.

"Not for sale, Nat. Now stop! I'm just letting you borrow these paints until you can replace yours. I wanted to replace them myself. But it's beter if you do it."

Nat sighed and put down his brushes. "Break time!" He slipped off his stool, landing on the ground, and stretched out beside her. "If you're going to be stubborn and won't sell, perhaps I should break in and steal it like that guy you told me about. What kind of jerk would bash up my paints like that?"

That was a good question, Kelcy thought. "I have no idea, and I'm really sorry about your paints. Did you order replacements yet? I want you to send me the bill."

"I have almost everything I need at the gallery, but Mrs. Dole gets the bill. She insisted. And I'll tell you one thing. I won't be bringing them out here again to be stored. I'd like to get my hands on that guy who messed up my stuff."

Kelcy shivered. "Well, he had his hands on me, and I can tell you it wasn't pleasant. He nearly suffocated me with that lacquer remover you had there. For a while we sold that stuff through the art-supply company I used to work for. But we quit handling it because of its volatility. Not many places do sell it anymore. Where did you get it?"

Nat looked baffled. "Kelcy, I don't know what you're talking about. I didn't have anything like that. Just paints, canvas, brushes. Not even turpentine. I use acrylics, as you know, that clean up with water."

"What are you saying? If that wasn't yours, Nat, then the intruder brought it in with him! It means he knew exactly what he was doing. Inhaling enough of those toxic fumes could be fatal. He might have been trying to kill me!" Her hands started trembling.

"Kelcy, get hold of yourself." Nat sat up, gently squeezing her arm. "Why would anyone want to kill you?"

He made her words sound so ridiculous, she

didn't know what to say. "Well, I don't know!" she snapped irritably. "Criminals don't need excuses nowadays for what they do."

Nat laughed softly. "Isn't it possible you had some of that stuff with your things and he accidentally found it?"

"No, it is not. I never used that stuff. And, furthermore, my things weren't touched. They were locked in my suitcase in the closet."

"Suppose the crook did bring it with him. He could have many uses in mind other than murder, like wiping prints off knobs or just knocking someone out for a time while he ransacked the place. There could be other uses that I haven't even thought of."

Kelcy looked away. "Oh, I suppose. You have a devious mind for that sort of thing, Nat."

"I'd prefer to say logical," he added lightheartedly.

She smiled faintly but quickly looked serious again. "But if Hawk hadn't heard me scream and come back when he did to get me away from those fumes, I could have died. I probably shouldn't say this, but you were his prime suspect."

"Me!" Nat appeared genuinely shocked. "Why me, for crying out loud? I wouldn't harm a fly. Do I look like a crook?"

"Remember, he doesn't know about the painting you're doing for Jenna, and I guess you don't fit his idea of a fence painter."

"Well, score one for him," Nat said sarcastically. "When's he coming back, anyway? I think it's best for all of us that I get this thing done quickly."

Kelcy shrugged. "I don't really know. He doesn't tell me anything. He was supposed to be back last night, but his aunt said he called to say his business was taking longer than he expected. She thought that meant he would be staying in the city a few more days. Why do you think Jenna has been asking you to come, wining and dining you the past two days so that you can work on the painting?"

"Hmmm, as a matter of fact, I did think it strange that you had all this free time to keep me company. When Westbrook's around, he keeps you slaving in his office. Ever think about quitting?"

Kelcy smiled wickedly. "All the time."

"In that case," Nat said seriously, "why don't you come to work for me at the gallery? So far I hired two assistants, but one's not all that reliable, and I sure could use the help, with the busy season starting next week and lasting till fall when we close. If you like the work and do good, Bennett has galleries all over. You could be transferred to his Florida gallery for the winter, if you want. He pays salary plus commission."

To Kelcy, the idea sounded good. "Are you serious? Just like that"—she snapped her fingers—"you'd give me a job?"

"I just said that, didn't I? You're a lot smarter than the two I already hired, and you know your stuff, lady. You could just be overqualified and grab my job if I'm not careful."

Kelcy gazed at the mill thoughtfully. "Can I have two weeks to think about it? I mean, I just can't up and leave here—well, for personal reasons—and I did promise Jenna to help with her July fifth festivities."

"No problem. Just come in when you're ready. Here, let's shake on the deal." Nat held out his hand. She took it firmly. "On second thought," he said, smiling wryly, "this will be better."

Nat gave her a lighthearted kiss on her cheek and mumbled something about a sealed bargain.

"Well, all right," Kelcy giggled. "You really think I'll be a good saleslady? I've never tried that type of work before."

Nat didn't answer, not right away. He was staring fixedly into the distance behind her.

"Blast it!" he said. "Now what are we going to do?"

Kelcy spun around. Her eyes widened as she saw Hawk Westbrook striding over the grassy field toward them. He was wearing a well-tailored dark business suit, tie and all, and he was approaching fast, looking angry.

"Nat," Kelcy whispered. "I'll tell him this is my painting and I'm just playing around with it. Remember you were painting the fence, not I, and you were on a break. It'll work!"

She quickly picked up a brush and started to stroke in the sky. If Nat didn't like it, he could always cover it later.

"Good thinking." Nat grinned.

There was something about Hawk's attitude, the way he regarded Kelcy appraisingly when he stopped at her side, that froze her into silence—a guilty silence which infuriated her because she had really done nothing wrong.

It was Nat who spoke at last as he lazily stretched. "Well, I'll get back to the fence then. Nice painting, Kelcy. Keep at it." He beamed. The glance he threw at her when he walked off was meant to indicate that he was finished for the day. Kelcy understood.

Hawk's dark gaze bored into the back of her head as he watched Kelcy slowly adding stroke after stroke. "With stacks of work piled up in the office, not to mention Jenna's harebrained plans needing organization, is that all you have to do, Miss Kendal? Idle away your time painting pictures. Take those things to the house and get back to the office. Right now!"

"In a minute," she answered, deliberately taking time with her brush, dipping it into water and cleaning it. Her courage was at its peak, although she wasn't going to test his temper too far. "You weren't really expected back until tomorrow, from what Jenna said."

"Ah, so that's it! While the cat's away, the mice will play." His gaze slipped over her sharply as she replaced the paint tubes in her case with time-consuming care. "Heaven knows I have enough on my mind without finding my secretary loafing in the grass, half dressed, with that good-for-nothing fence painter. He should have finished long ago and been on his way."

Kelcy angrily snapped her paint case shut. "It's not my fault you're in a bad mood, Mr. Westbrook! I finished everything you gave me to do. Your letters are waiting for your signature—or did you expect me to forge your name to them? And I've been working with your aunt all morning. I came out here to relax. As a matter of fact, she sent me!"

"Playtime is over, Miss Kendal. Now get back to the office."

She slipped on her shoes, folded the stool, put it and the canvas under one arm, and picked up her paint case. "Yes, sir, I shall be there shortly," she replied, the expression on her face belying the submissiveness of her words.

Forty minutes had elapsed by the time she entered the office. It should have taken her only half that time, but she had been slow in changing into her most modest dress, a simple cotton print with a high neckline.

"Do you find this outfit more appropriate, Mr. Westbrook?" Kelcy asked icily.

"I hardly think you want me to answer that—unless you're fishing for compliments."

"If I had that in mind," she responded dryly, "I wouldn't bother to ask you."

"Good. I'm sure you can always find some man like Collins who will tell you what you want to hear." His voice sounded cool and indifferent on the surface, but beneath lay a smoldering contempt —almost as if he was jealous.

"Since you've finished that batch of letters, you can work on this annual report." He handed her a thick booklet.

Kelcy looked at it with confusion. "What exactly am I supposed to do with this, Mr. Westbrook, read it?"

He looked at her with a piercing dark glint that made her uneasy. "Yes, read it, every word, and outline the contents—from the chairman's message to the Biggs Company ten-year financial summary. I want it typed into a condensed form for review."

She stared at him as if he had gone mad. "But, Mr. Westbrook, you know as well as I do this is last year's report on the company. They sent you current information which I've already programmed into the computer. I can have an updated printout on your desk in five minutes."

An ironic smile lit up his face. "Can you? I'm pleased to hear it. Now do the assignment I gave you."

Assignment. That was a good word, all right, Kelcy thought as she began the tedious outline. She felt like a schoolgirl doing her lesson—no, like a schoolgirl being punished for lateness or playing hooky or somesuch thing.

She was seething as Hawk walked through her office to the file cabinet to return a folder he had previously taken out.

In a sarcastic tone just loud enough for him to hear, Kelcy mumbled, "I wonder if he expects me to outline the pictures, too!"

Suddenly his dark face loomed above her, his expression sinister. "Are you questioning my orders, Miss Kendal?"

"No, I'm doing just as I was told. But you know as well as I do this outline doesn't need to be typed today, tomorrow—or ever! You were just—oh, forget it!"

He pulled her up from her chair. "Just what, Kelcy?" he asked. His strong fingers forced her chin upward, almost gently, so that her green eyes would have to meet his.

She trembled at the touch, at the sheer masculine strength of him. "You were just angry that your aunt gave me some time off and for once I was actually enjoying myself!"

"Enjoying yourself, eh?" he rasped. "Cuddling up to that fence-painter idiot! If that's your idea of enjoyment, Kelcy, you come to me. I'll show you enjoyment in a man's arms like you've never known." His hand slid from her face, holding her firmly against him.

Kelcy tried to pull away from him, but he was too strong for her. In the next second, she felt his lips, warm and demanding, kissing hers, destroying any will she had left to resist him.

As he held her in his arms, she tried to tell herself she hated him, but her senses clearly told her that wasn't so. She had fallen in love with Hawk Westbrook. The truth, though maddening, was undeniable. Yet it was all so pointless. It could only lead to her unhappiness, she was convinced. Hawk would never love her in return. He was just playing his mocking games, and she would be a fool to think otherwise.

She was saved, at least temporarily, from her own betraying emotions when the phone rang. Only then did his mouth leave hers, and he pushed her away almost roughly.

"Kelcy," he snapped huskily, "I didn't mean to do that. You provoked me, but that's no excuse. Answer the blasted phone!"

It was difficult for Kelcy to think straight. Rather

desperately she tried to pull herself together. For one heart-stopping moment he reached out and cupped the curve of her chin in the palm of his hand, stroking it gently before walking back into his office. Her hand trembling, she picked up the phone.

"Westbrook Industries," she said breathlessly.

"Kelcy, honey, it's me—Glen! What took you so long to answer? Don't tell me old Hawk has you downstairs sacking grain during coffee breaks."

"Glen!" She relaxed slightly, looking at Hawk's closed door. "I hope you called to say you're ready to tell your cousin the truth."

There was a pause. "Actually—well, I'll get to that later. How do you like the house?"

"It's lovely," she said honestly.

"Good. I knew you'd like it. Then you won't mind too much staying on a bit longer."

Kelcy sighed. "Oh, no, Glen. Three weeks is what I promised you—that's it! The place itself is charming but not your cousin!"

Laughter came over the telephone line. "Ah, Kelcy, what's the matter? The boss working you too hard? I'm not surprised. Hawk is most disagreeable whenever he's closing a business deal. We all try to avoid him like the plague then. Things should lighten up now that he has everything settled."

"Lighten up! You must be kidding! He'll never lighten up. Right now he has me sitting here outlining the Biggs Company annual report from last year!"

Glen laughed again. "Now you stop kidding me, Kelcy! He bought out Biggs last night. I was with him and witnessed the transaction. Actually that's why I need more time . . . to tie up some loose ends. How about giving me another week?"

"No!" she said firmly. "Please tell him the truth, Glen. I can't take very much more of this!"

"All right, calm down, honey. How about agreeing to this? Jenna invited me up for this July fifth shindig she's planning. I'll drive up there and tell him in person that night. Surely those few more days won't make a difference to you, but they will for me. What do you say?"

Kelcy thought that over. "I don't know, Glen. Our agreement was three weeks."

"Or so. I remember saying exactly that. Or something like that, anyway. And you wouldn't want to disappoint Jenna. She told me how much she likes you and what a help you've been to her since you arrived. On the fifth I'll straighten everything out. You have my word."

"Glen, you never play fair," Kelcy blurted out.

"That must mean you're giving me the few extra days. You're a sweetheart, Kelcy."

"I really shouldn't, but I will for your aunt's sake—hers only. I hope I'm making that clear."

"You are. Now can I talk to Hawk? I've got some news that will put him in a good mood."

After she made Glen promise that he would definitely come on the fifth with a full confession, she transferred the call to Hawk's office. Several minutes later he walked through the door, his jacket slung over one shoulder, the tie he had been wearing dangling from his pocket. He stopped at her desk.

"Scrap that outline," he said with a keen glance at her pale cheeks. "You've had enough for today. Go find Jenna if you like. She has some old photos she wanted to show you. And about before—well, it's a long drive up from the city. I'm tired and I guess I lost my temper. Let's lock this place up, and I'll walk you back to the house."

Kelcy looked at him in astonishment. Could she have heard him right? Was he apologizing? She couldn't be sure. He did not speak again, and they walked in silence to the house. As they reached the kitchen door, he opened it and she thanked him.

Once they were in the hallway outside her room, Hawk gave her a level glance, then turned to continue to the main part of the house. She watched his departure, whispering softly, "What did Glen have to say to you, Hawk Westbrook?"

But there was no way she could find out. She resolutely put it out of her mind, then changed into comfortable jeans and set off to find Jenna.

# CHAPTER TWELVE

The days that followed flew by quickly because Kelcy had plenty to do. In the morning she worked on routine matters for Hawk in the mill office, rarely seeing him. In the afternoons and evenings she had an enjoyable time assisting Jenna with the open house and ball preparations.

Insisting Kelcy was more talented than anyone she could hire, Jenna put her in charge of decorations. Under Kelcy's direction, with help from Sue and her housekeeping staff, the house was transformed into a nineteenth-century showplace. The actual manual labor was completed in record time with two days to spare.

Around eleven A.M. on July third, Kelcy was busy with last-minute touches—tying bows to the stair railings while at the same time memorizing her tour speech—when Jenna brought in the mail.

"Oh, my! Advance ticket sales have already doubled our expectations," the old woman said brightly as she looked over the report she had just received. "Perhaps we should make this an annual event." She handed Kelcy a letter. "This is for you, dear."

Kelcy thought it might be from her friend Sandra. She was very surprised to see it had come from the law firm that had handled her parents' estate. She opened it and read through it quickly.

"Oh, for heaven's sake! I can hardly believe this," she exclaimed.

"What is it, dear?" Jenna asked absently.

"The lawyers that represented my parents' estate found my name on the state treasurer's list of abandoned property, and they're notifying me that I have a savings account of almost five thousand dollars to be claimed. I knew Mom had opened an account for me when I was a baby, but I thought my great-aunt, Bess, had gotten control of that when she became my guardian. I thought it was all used up. But I guess she couldn't touch it."

"How nice for you, Kelcy," Jenna said sweetly.

"For you, too, Jenna. Now I can pay you back for those clothes that were charged to your account."

Jenna put her finger to her chin. For a second she looked puzzled, as if she had forgotten all about them. "Oh, the lovely suit and things! Well, actually you don't owe me anything. You see—well, never mind that now—we'll talk about it later."

"You bet we will," a deep voice drawled from above them on the stairs.

Kelcy and Jenna both looked up to find Hawk on the landing.

"For heaven's sake, Hawk," Jenna scolded. "Why are you hovering about up there, frightening the wits out of us?"

He laughed softly. "I was just on my way down from the ballroom, thinking how crazy I must be to let you talk me into allowing this. And the lady from the catering service wants to see you up there now, Jenna." He walked down toward them.

"Yes, yes, Hawk, I was just on my way up. Did you hear about Kelcy's windfall?" she asked, passing him on the steps.

"I heard."

When Jenna was out of earshot, he said as he suddenly whipped out a slip of paper from his back pocket, "Now let's talk about this, shall we?"

Kelcy looked at it inquisitively. "Well, what is it?"

He held it up for her to read. "What's the idea of charging a new outfit to my account? That's some nerve, young lady!"

"B-but I didn't!" Kelcy cried, aghast.

"Didn't you? Then explain this."

Kelcy swallowed, not knowing what to say. She recognized the name of the shop and the items listed as being those she had purchased. "I went in that store with Jenna under protest. I just wanted to buy a cheap pair of jogging shoes somewhere else, but she insisted I try on these other things. And before I knew it, she and the clerk both were talking me into buying them. I said I couldn't afford to, but Jenna said you paid your employees well and to consider it an investment. I could hardly tell her any salary I do make goes to pay off your car-repair bill."

"So for spite, you decided to charge those things to my account instead!"

"No. When I told her again I really couldn't afford those things, she didn't seem to care and told me she would charge them to her own account and that I should pay her when I had the money."

The skepticism showed in his eyes. "Sometimes Jenna does use my account when she forgets hers, but then where are her other charges? All I see here are these things in a size she could never get into."

Kelcy gazed at the slip. He was right. Only her suit, blouse, and shoes were charged to his account. "I don't know!"

"Don't know? You have that innocent act rehearsed well, Miss Kendal."

"For the last time, I do not know," she said hotly. "Jenna asked me to bring the car around to the store while the clerk was writing up her slip and wrapping the packages. Unless, well, maybe there were separate charge slips and the other didn't come through yet."

"Hmm, yes, maybe," he mocked.

Kelcy's eyes flashed green fire. "Well, you needn't worry about the money. I can pay for those things when I close out my savings account. And if that isn't soon enough, I'll take everything back. The shop has a liberal return policy. I made sure of that. And since I haven't opened any of the boxes—except the one for the shoes—I think that's what I'll do. Just give me that charge slip and I'll take care of it."

When she grabbed for the paper, he held it out of her reach. "You don't like the clothes then?"

"Of course, I like the clothes. Who wouldn't?" she snapped.

"Then what is it? Don't they fit?"

"They fit perfectly, Mr. Westbrook. Now may I please have that slip?"

But instead of handing it to her, he stuffed it back into his pocket. "Then keep them," he ordered. "Jenna's not usually extravagant. Obviously she thought your wardrobe was lacking."

Hawk's aunt not extravagant! Kelcy was going to set him straight about that. "Perhaps Jenna's shopping style does not seem extravagant to you, a man who wears and can afford eight-hundred-dollar suits. But she's no bargain hunter. I can tell you that. I had even thought of suggesting that you keep your credit cards out of her reach. But that is none of my business. However, the clothes she charged for me are. I won't keep them! I can return them with or without that slip." Her pride had been hurt enough.

"You will keep them," he ordered with authority, "and wear them tomorrow night if they're suitable. My aunt has included you in our dinner plans for a late meal before we watch the fireworks display over the bay. The charges on that bill I have decided to add to the amount you already owe me, which will be deducted from your salary. Be careful, Miss Kendal. At this rate you'll be working for me for the rest of your life."

Kelcy narrowed her eyes. The matter was closed. She could read it in the set of Hawk's jaw as he turned to go. She wasn't going to argue either, for there would be no point. Glen was coming the day after tomorrow, and then Charles Hawken Westbrook would be eating all his nasty words.

The fifth of July came in with a misty breeze right off the lake. It cleared into lovely sunshine by the time the first visitors arrived at the house. According to plan, they were greeted on the front porch by Jenna, wearing a long blue gown with many bows and ribbons. There she gave a short welcoming speech, handed out programs, and stamped tickets while herding guests into small groups for the actual home tour.

At that point they were handed over to either Sue or Kelcy, also in historic costumes. From basement to ballroom, the young women did their best to inform the many people about the architectural styling and the furnishings, especially the antiques, answering questions whenever possible. On completion of the house tour, all visitors were invited to relax on the terrace where they could sit and enjoy cakes, cookies, and beverages served by Mrs. Meinert and the housekeeping staff. After that they could stroll through the garden or visit the arts-and-crafts exhibition on the way to the mill.

Carriages were supplied by the stables, driven by Brad and his helpers, to shuttle guests around the grounds. And Hawk himself personally guided all visitors through the lower portion of the mill.

So it went from nine to five, a steady stream of

interested people viewing, listening, asking questions, and simply enjoying themselves in the warm, pleasant weather. When the last of the tourists had left and the artists packed up and gone, the volunteer helpers were rounded up and served a delicious buffet-style dinner before they began preparations for the evening ball.

Kelcy was snapping a picture of Brad and Sue seated in one of the carriages in front of the house when Jenna came out to watch them.

"Well, that is so perfect." She smiled brightly. "Thanks to all of you, we had a very successful day. It was so lovely. We can only hope the evening goes as well."

Everyone agreed with her. Sue stepped out of the carriage just as Guthrie raced by. The dog was glad to be free since he had spent the day confined in his kennel. Hawk was not far behind him and came walking around the house toward them.

Sue waved to him. "Come here, master of the mill," she teased. "I want to take your picture in that stuffy old-fashioned outfit."

"What should I do, just stand here?" he asked.

"No. Why don't you get up in the carriage? You, too, Kelcy. I don't have any pictures of you yet either. Brad, you come down here and show me how this thing works." She took the camera from Kelcy.

"Here," Kelcy offered, "I'll show you. Set the distance and—"

"No, no, let Brad show me. You get up next to Hawk in the carriage and no back talk."

"Yes, do, Kelcy," Jenna urged her.

She knew she was outnumbered. Reluctantly she climbed up next to Hawk, who was seated with the reins in one hand.

'Oh, don't look so stiff, Hawk," Jenna ordered as Brad explained meter readings to Sue. "Put your arm around that girl and look happy."

Kelcy cringed inwardly when she felt Hawk's hand rest on her shoulder, then pull her snugly to his side. "How's this?" he laughed.

"Perfect." Jenna smiled.

"I knew she would say that," Kelcy commented absently.

"What was that?" Hawk whispered dangerously close to her ear.

Sue aimed the camera. "Smile. Come on, Kelcy . . . Good."

Kelcy turned to Hawk. "Okay, she's got it. You can remove your hand."

"Shush! Hey, Brad! Your boys were looking for you in the kitchen. Why don't you go in and find them and have some more to eat. There's plenty left. I'll take the horse and buggy back to the barn."

"Sure, go ahead," Brad said. "Jenna, Sue, how about you coming, too? That way I won't feel like a hog going in by myself." He stepped between the two ladies, took each by the arm, and started walking them in that direction.

With a gentle flick of his hand, Hawk started the horse off on a slow, plodding gait.

Kelcy reached for the reins, touching his hand briefly. "Wait, I want to get down."

His glance slid over her sharply. "Stay put and enjoy the ride. I haven't seen you all day and I wanted to thank you for all the help you gave Jenna, and for taking her to the parade, dinner, and the fireworks yesterday. She said she had a good time. Sorry, I couldn't make it after all, but something came up." He removed his hand from around her, placing it across the back of her seat.

Kelcy inched away from him. "I didn't mind. I'm very fond of Jenna." She was surprised that he had bothered to thank her at all. That was a side of him she didn't know existed. In fact, she almost became suspicious. "I had a nice time myself," she added quietly.

"And you're thinking it was even nicer because I wasn't there." Hawk smiled wryly.

Caught off guard by his light mood, she smiled. "Well, maybe." But what she really had been thinking was that she wasn't used to polite conversations with him, and it was confusing her. She wasn't sure she knew how to react.

Hawk was silent then for a long while. The clopping of the horse's hooves, the odd bird calling to his companions, the humming of insects in the grass all blended together into the hypnotic, soothing sounds of the country. Kelcy felt a part of the place, as if she belonged there beside the man she loved. But he would never know. The night would pass and she would leave in the morning. For once Glen told his cousin the truth, there would be no reason for her to stay.

"You know, you're expected to play your part tonight," Hawk said lazily, breaking into her thoughts.

Kelcy nodded. "Margaret Emma Dumont, the

first mistress of Hawk's Mill. Yes, I know, it was
Jenna's idea. I'll be wearing a reproduction of one
of her gowns. We've been sewing costumes all
week, patterning styles after photos and paintings
found in the Historical Society's collection. And
you'll be taking the part of Fred Herman Dumont,
first master of the mill."

He smiled mockingly. "I know. Have you read
the history of those two?"

Kelcy nodded again. "Highly romanticized, I'd
say. At her betrothal party, Margaret Emma meets
young Dumont for the first time. After one dance,
they fall madly in love. He sweeps her off her feet,
carries her in his arms from her Green Bay home
into the night to elope, leaving behind one shocked
fiance and all of her family. I can't really imagine
such an event ever happening."

"Love works in mysterious ways, they say,
Kelcy." Hawk grinned.

She met his eyes, feeling tense with her private
thoughts. "Yes," she answered, looking away. "I
suppose you're right."

# CHAPTER THIRTEEN

Her fingers resting lightly on Hawk's arm, Kelcy strolled into the ballroom. She was in full costume in her embroidered white gown with its long flared skirt decorated at the bottom by flounces edged in lace and white satin rosettes. Large puff sleeves billowed from a trim-fitting bodice. Her shiny chestnut hair was pulled away from her face with curls cascading softly at the back, adorned by satin ribbon and more rosettes. Hawk wore a handsomely tailored black suit that had once belonged to his grandfather. As they entered, playing their parts of host and hostess, everyone cheered and clapped.

Hawk slipped a corsage of red, white, and blue-tinted tea roses on her wrist, kissed her lightly on the cheek, and made a short welcoming speech, thus officially opening the evening festivities.

Kelcy glanced around the room, studying the

lighting, the decorations, the guests in costumes, and knew Jenna would be saying "it's perfect." For once she had to agree. And where was Jenna? she wondered, looking over the crowd until she spotted her dancing in front of the bandstand. Her partner was a very distinguished older man.

Sue and Brad came up just then to greet her.

"Kelcy, you look gorgeous!" Sue complimented. "So does Hawk. We did a great job fixing this place up, didn't we?"

"It turned out nice." Kelcy smiled. "You two look the handsome couple yourselves. Why aren't you dancing?"

"We will later. Truthfully I'm kind of tired from giving all those tours today, but I see Jenna's out there." Sue giggled. "Why aren't you and Hawk— oh, I see he's busy talking to that beautiful blonde over there. Who is she?"

Kelcy glanced where Sue was staring. And Sue couldn't have been more right. The woman Hawk was talking to was indeed beautiful. Her honey-blond hair and pale, flawless skin were lovely, as was the lilac formal she wore. When the young woman glanced over in their direction and smiled, Kelcy quickly turned away, feeling self-conscious.

"I don't know who she is," Kelcy answered moodily.

It was then that she spied Glen, Hawk's cousin, ordering a drink at the bar. "Excuse me, Sue, Brad, there's someone I must talk to."

"Sure," Brad replied. "Well, Sue, let's try this dance to see if I can remember how." He took his wife by the hand, and their voices trailed off as they moved among the dancers.

Kelcy inched her way through the guests, stopping once or twice to speak with women who were curious about her costume, until she reached the bar. "Glen, you're here. I was beginning to think you weren't coming."

His blue eyes lit up when he turned and saw her. "Kelcy, honey, long time no see. You look beautiful!" He gave her a big hug and nearly spilled his drink. "Life up here sure must agree with you. The last time I saw you, you were as pale as a ghost." He reached out and brushed back some hair from her forehead. "Good, no scars from that automatic garage-door transmitter Hawk had clipped to his sun visor."

She blinked. "Is that what struck me? I never knew. Since then, I've been in his car and haven't seen or noticed any transmitter clipped there."

"That's what hit you, honey. If it hadn't been for that, you wouldn't have had a scratch. I walked away and you could have, too. When Hawk discovered what zonked you, that next day he had it mounted under the dash. After cursing a blue streak, I might add."

Kelcy touched Glen's arm. "You have to tell him now, Glen, the truth about that night. You promised."

Glen grinned boyishly. Putting down his drink, he took Kelcy's hand and guided it up to his shoulder. "Now? Oh, no, Kelcy, not now. It's too early to spoil this fine party. I'll tell him later. Now I want to dance with you."

She really didn't have much choice. Before she could open her mouth to protest, he had whisked her out on the floor with the other dancers. After they'd taken several turns around the room, the music stopped and the band leader asked everyone to exchange partners. After that, Kelcy lost all track of time. She got caught up in fun, mixing with the other guests, posing for pictures, assisting Jenna and some of the other Historical Society members with minor duties.

As the evening wore on, she grew tired from all the activity. Grabbing a glass of lemonade and a slice of chocolate cake, Kelcy found a chair in a corner and sat down. She had seen Hawk throughout the evening dancing with that woman and others or talking with guests. Once or twice their eyes had met in startling awareness, but he appeared to be ignoring her as much as she tried to ignore him. She was relieved by that, she supposed.

"Hi, is anyone sitting here?" a soft voice asked.

Kelcy looked up, startled to see the blonde Hawk had been with earlier. Her eyes were an unusual shade of violet, her smile cheerful, and Kelcy felt guilty for her previous jealous thoughts. "No—no one."

The girl sat down. "I just wanted to tell you that I think your costume is stunning. I heard you cut and sewed it yourself—how talented! I have a hard time sewing a straight seam. Are you a professional dress designer or artist or anything?"

Kelcy smiled, cringing inwardly. Why did the

girl have to be so nice? Couldn't she be rude or haughty or have some other flaws?

"Thank you. Actually I have an art degree, but I haven't had much chance to use it. I learned to sew from necessity, I'm afraid. I'm working temporarily as Mr. Westbrook's secretary."

"Oh, you're Hawk's secretary!" she smiled brightly. "I should have guessed because I was told he picked himself a green-eyed beauty. I hope we can be friends. I'm Stephanie Davis—Mr. Westbrook's fiancee. It's still a secret. He's going to tell his family tonight, but he gave me the ring last night."

His fiancee! The words echoed in her ears as Kelcy stared dazedly at the sparkling diamond the girl held out to show her.

So that was where Hawk had been last night—with Stephanie. Catching her breath, Kelcy took a sip of lemonade in the hopes of steadying her voice.

"Congratulations. I wish you every happiness. Please excuse me. I have something I really must do."

Kelcy put down her glass and unfinished cake, knowing her brusque behavior was most impolite. Yet she had to get away from Stephanie.

What would she do now? She could no longer stay in this house loving Hawk the way she did and knowing he was engaged to another woman. The pain was beyond endurance. She had wanted to be there when Glen told Hawk the truth about his car. But even that didn't matter anymore. Besides, she was almost convinced Glen was never going to make that confession to his cousin.

Kelcy didn't know how she could manage to get away, but she was determined to leave Hawk's house now, even if she had to stand with her suitcases in the road and hitchhike. She slipped down the stairs, carefully avoiding everyone she knew. And there at the bottom she saw her answer—Nat Collins was standing in the entry way talking to Ivan Palmer and one of the security guards assigned to the front door. She went up to them boldly.

"Excuse me, gentlemen," she said. "I wish to talk to Mr. Collins for a moment." She grabbed Nat's arm and led him past the roped-in area to the quiet hall.

He looked surprised. "What's up?"

"Am I glad to see you!" She smiled. "I don't know why you're here, but I'm sure glad you are."

"I was—Kelcy, is something wrong? You look flushed."

"Is that gallery job offer still good?"

Nat nodded. "You know it is."

"Fine, I'll take it. I want to leave here now, tonight. You said I could rent a room above the gallery. All I have to do is get my things. Can we go right away?"

He gazed at her, confused. "Well, I guess. But Mrs. Dole wanted me on hand to unveil my painting. She plans on presenting it to her nephew at the ball later on." He read the anxiety in Kelcy's eyes and decided she truly needed his help. "But I don't suppose it makes much difference if I'm here or not." He paused, looking her up and down. "Don't you want to change first?"

"Later, Nat. I just want to get out of here."

Nat Collins didn't say another word, perhaps because he didn't know what to say. He simply nodded and followed Kelcy to her room where she took her already packed suitcases and tote bag out of the closet. Gallantly he picked them up. She grabbed her small violet from the dresser top, looked around the room for the last time to commit it to memory, and started for the door.

Two steps later she stopped in her tracks as the door flew open and Hawk thundered in. He took one look at Nat, his eyes noting Kelcy's luggage in his hands before they rested on Kelcy herself, her face ashen, her fingers gripping the little flower pot for dear life.

Without thinking, Nat moved to block Hawk's way, standing directly in front of him.

With one arm, Hawk brushed him aside warning him:

"Look, Collins, I didn't come here to mix it up with you, but I will if I have to. Stay out of this or you'll never know what hit you!"

Nat backed off. He liked Kelcy and would have done almost anything for her. But he wasn't about to challenge Westbrook in his own home. It just wasn't wise.

"So why don't you leave us alone," Hawk went on.

"NO!" Kelcy cried. "Please, Nat, stay! He wouldn't dare try anything violent in front of a witness."

Both men turned to stare at her.

"What the devil's wrong with you, Kelcy?" Hawk demanded angrily. "I didn't come here to hurt you. Heaven's sake, woman, I just want to talk to you. You hardly gave me a chance tonight. And you're not running out on our contract."

Kelcy gazed at him mutinously. Courage was in her favor. "That contract is no good, Hawk. My three weeks are up! Glen should have told you long before this. It's not my fault that he didn't. And I can assure you there's nothing I want to talk to you about."

"Maybe not, but I want to say plenty to you."

"If it's about your fiancee," she said, "I don't want to hear. Good luck to her!"

Hawk frowned. "What?"

Nat Collins edged to the hall door, having put down the bags. "I think I'll just stroll up to the ballroom if nobody minds. Ah, Kelcy, I think you can take care of yourself, and it couldn't possibly hurt to hear the man out."

Kelcy looked betrayed and was about to protest. So much for Nat's support. How two-faced could anyone be? Now he was siding with Hawk. Well, it didn't make any difference. It would be harder, of course, but with or without Nat's help, she was leaving. She watched him close the door as he walked out.

Kelcy took several steps, planning to follow after him. Hawk had other ideas. He caught her arm and dragged her around to face him.

"Look out!" she snapped. "I almost dropped my violet!"

"Forget that stupid plant. Now who did you wish good luck to just before?"

"Your fiancee! Have you forgotten Stephanie already?"

His brows shot up. "Stephanie Davis? No, I haven't forgotten her, but what makes you think she's my fiancee?"

"She told me, Hawk!"

"She told you we were engaged? Why the devil would she say that?"

With a cool bitterness in her voice, Kelcy replied. "Probably because it's true. I saw her ring. And she said, 'I'm Mr. Westbrook's fiancee.' What kind of man are you, anyway, trying to deny such a thing?"

Hawk laughed. "So that's it!"

He actually thought he was amusing! The arrogant swine! "Let go of me, Hawk. I'm leaving."

He was still laughing. "You're not going anywhere, you hear!"

There was a sudden draft of wind. The hall door opened slowly, and footsteps were heard.

"No one seems to be going anywhere, I'm afraid," Nat said.

Without turning around, Hawk growled, "Collins, I thought you were going upstairs."

"I thought I was, too, but this guy had other plans. You don't think I'm dumb enough to get involved in a lovers' quarrel by choice."

"Shut up!" a harsh voice ordered. "Get over by the others. My business is with Kelcy. Give me what I want, girl, and no one gets hurt."

At first no one moved. They stood transfixed, the full realization of what they heard not yet registering. Then as Hawk whirled around and Nat edged into the room, Kelcy caught sight of a short black-haired man with a beard. He was standing there, a triumphant smile on his face, holding a gun in his hand.

"Sir, I don't think we've ever met," she began. "If this is a joke, it's not at all funny."

But the man laughed anyway. "Oh, you know me all right. Look closer."

"Sir, I—your voice, it does sound—James Miles!" Kelcy gasped. She stared at the man incredulously. "B-but your hair and that beard—and they said you were in South America!"

"And I would be too if it wasn't for you."

All eyes were on Kelcy.

"Me? Why me?" she asked.

"I want that paint set I gave you. Get it!"

Kelcy shook her head with disbelief. "Good grief, Mr. Miles! You have a set just like it. And despite that painter's vest you're wearing, you'll never convince me you're an aspiring artist."

"Had a set, you little idiot! I had one. You now have it. That day I was switching paints, I must have accidentally switched cases, too."

"But they're identical."

"Except for the fact mine has a hidden key that unlocks a certain safety-deposit box containing all my Swiss bank account numbers. Without it, my dear, my millions are useless to me. Hand it over."

"Kelcy," Nat cut in. "I don't know what this is all about, but why don't you give it to him? Considering he has a gun and all, it might be best for all of us."

She glanced at Nat, who appeared nervous, then

at Hawk, who was just the opposite—cool, intimidating, thinking, no doubt, that she was to blame for all of this. Even Miles seemed to respect Hawk in his odd sort of way. James Miles. She looked at him coldly, noting the missing pocket on his vest.

"You broke in here that night, destroyed Nat's paints, and nearly killed me, didn't you?" Kelcy snapped.

"Brilliant guess. If I had found those paints in my own kit, I wouldn't be here now."

"Ah, what's a few paints, Kelcy? I have others," Nat said jokingly.

Kelcy scowled at him. "Nat, please stay out of this. Miles, Hawk's dog had a piece of your vest. Did he attack you?"

James Miles's lip curled. "That dog, he's lucky I didn't see him around tonight, or he'd be history. You'll be history, too, if you don't get that set."

Perhaps Kelcy didn't realize the danger she was in, or perhaps she just didn't care. She set her chin defiantly. "I'm not going to help you, Miles. Do yourself a favor and give yourself up."

James Miles turned livid. "I'm warning you, Kelcy. I'll use this gun. Now get that case."

Nat spoke up quickly. "It's got to be around here somewhere, fella. I know she still has it. Ah, in one of those suitcases I'll bet."

Kelcy sighed, exasperated. "Why don't you just get it for him, Nat?"

She saw Miles's hand tense around the gun and then relax. His mouth curved cruelly, his laugh was harsh. "Not a bad idea. Go ahead. Find it for me, young man."

For one short second Nat exchanged glances with Hawk, then started for the suitcases. What happened next was a blur of chaos—suitcases sliding across the floor, fists flying, men shouting, a gun shooting. Kelcy felt her flower pot shatter as it pushed into her ribs. She fell backward from the impact, crumbling to the floor. And she found herself gasping for breath.

Suddenly Hawk was at her side, carefully running his fingers over her ribs. He slid his arm around her and effortlessly eased her forward. It felt just right. She could breathe comfortably again.

He whispered softly, "Oh, Kelcy, thank God that bullet bounced off your plant." His tone sounded husky and weary. "There's a limit to what I can take."

"Miles shot my violet, Hawk—my violet!" She began to laugh shakily.

Touching her cheek gently, he said, "And I think it will make it with some water. You, too, but you might have a few bruised ribs."

She smiled at him. Just then a scuffling sound caught her attention. Kelcy turned her head slightly to see Nat pull James Miles up from the floor where he'd had him pinned. Miles was handcuffed. She was utterly bewildered. Where had Nat gotten those? she wondered.

"Are you all right, Kelcy?" he asked before slipping out a concealed shoulder gun.

She nodded, still trembling. "I think so. But . . . I don't understand. Why were you carrying that gun, Nat?"

"Let Hawk explain. He was in on it from the beginning."

Through tear-stained eyes she watched several uniformed security officers enter the hall and come to Nat's assistance. He didn't seem to need them. He was cool and calm and very much in control now. She glanced up at Hawk.

"It's over, Kelcy," he said softly. He swung her up in his arms and set her on her feet, pulling her close. "Don't you ever scare me like that again."

She took comfort in the shelter of his arms. She didn't know why he was being so understanding, and she didn't care. All she wanted was to be held and protected.

Hawk was grinning at her.

"Thank heaven for Collins. That's all I can say." Over her head, he called, "Nat, you're not such a bad guy to have around—sometimes."

Nat was grinning, too. "You're not so bad your-self, Westbrook. She could do worse—and I get your meaning. Come on, guys. Let's get Miles out of here. I'm sorry, Kelcy, but I'll need to take your case for evidence, and you might be asked for state-ments later."

When everyone had left, Kelcy eased out of Hawk's arms. It was just the moment of shock, she told herself, that had made her stay there so long. Now she was back in control. "So, Mr. Westbrook, explain. I guess Nat wasn't a gallery manager after all."

"Undercover agent. I can't say I care much for his tactics, but he did get the job done. He had been trailing Miles and could have nabbed him at any time. The guy wasn't too smart. However, Nat was waiting, trying to find out where he had stashed the money. When he did—well, you saw the rest."

She certainly had. Things were becoming clearer every minute. "You were in on all this?"

Hawk ran impatient fingers through his hair. "I was—Jenna, too, even Glen to some extent. You see, I was sort of recruited. The day I agreed to hire you, I did some checking, I have some police connections. And the police investigators had a hunch Miles was following you. They asked me to help them and put me in touch with Collins to set up a plan. I agreed. But I can tell you one thing. I wouldn't do it again knowing the danger you were in."

Sighing, she said, "Well, Mr. Westbrook, you all got what you wanted. What now? Can I go?" Her hand came up to brush away tears that had misted her eyes.

"Why suddenly Mr. Westbrook?" he asked. "It was Hawk before in my arms. And, no, you can't go anywhere. There's still that little matter of a debt you owe me."

"Oh, stop it!" Kelcy begged, remembering those precious moments she would always treasure. And just then she also remembered he was engaged to Stephanie. "I don't owe you anything. I had nothing to do with stealing your car. It was Glen. And I can tell from that arrogant smile plastered on your face, you knew that, too, all along."

Hawk was laughing now. "No, Kelcy, actually I didn't. Not at the first instant. But I caught on fast that you were covering up for him. Glen gave himself away. It was most unlike him to go that far out of his way to find me. In fact, it's unlike him to go out of his way for anything unless it's in his own interests. You ought to be ashamed of yourself, Kelcy, for such deception," he added mockingly. "Look at the hell I put you through. You were in over your head from the start. I hope you learned your lesson."

She faced him squarely. "I ought to be ashamed of myself? You should talk? So all along you were playing games with me. I knew it! I hope you enjoyed yourself!"

"Oh, I did. Believe me, I did!"

Kelcy's face flamed with anger. "What I still don't understand is, if you suspected Glen, why did you let him get away with it?"

He gazed into her flashing eyes. "I don't know. Curiosity, maybe. I wanted to see what he was up to. I thought you were in love with him. It was the first time I ever envied Glen anything." He smiled wryly. "Why did you agree to help him, Kelcy? Do you love him?"

She looked down at her fingers, fidgeting with the corsage on her wrist. "No! I don't know why I didn't tell on him. I must have been crazy with shock. In a way, though, it's your own fault. Your arrogant personality—accusing me of all sorts of horrid things. I guess something inside me snapped, and I just wanted to get even. Get even!" She laughed softly. "It sure sounds stupid now. I don't suppose if I apologized, Hawk, that you'd—"

"Try it, Kelcy. You little thief."

Her eyes grew wide. "I'm not a thief! Haven't you heard a word I said?"

"Aren't you? What do you call it then?" Hawk grabbed her shoulders and gave her a gentle shake. "I'm not talking about any car. I'm talking about something a lot more valuable to me than that!"

"Let go of me," Kelcy demanded. "I didn't steal anything of yours."

"No? You stole my heart, Kelcy!"

His arms circled around her. He drew her so close to him that she could feel the warmth and strength of him. His lips covered hers possessively —hungry kisses, yet softly tender, as though he had been waiting forever to kiss her.

Suddenly he lifted his head, stared into her misty eyes, and whispered huskily, "Kelcy, I love you. I think I have ever since I saw that frightened green-eyed girl in that hospital bed. I went through a maelstrom of emotions that night, fighting it all the way, right until tonight when I felt like punching out every man who danced with you. Will you forgive me for acting like an arrogant idiot with you all these weeks?"

She looked up at him, unable to speak for a moment. "How can you stand there saying that to me with Stephanie, your fiancee, just upstairs?"

He squeezed her to him and laughed. "Is that all you can say to me?"

"Yes!" she snapped.

"Well, I'm not the only Mr. Westbrook around, Kelcy. Did you ever think about Glen?"

"Are you saying—"

"Stephanie is engaged to Glen. Heaven help her.

That night he was joyriding in my car, he was supposed to be taking the final exam—a late make-up exam at that—to complete his MBA. He wasn't sure he'd pass, so he hired someone to take his place, and he left the campus. According to our grandfather's will, you see, we weren't allowed our inheritance until we received our MBA's and worked for the company, which he did. He's got the inheritance now by hook and crook—that's Cousin Glen. He never was interested in the family company, however. He wanted the money to set up his own business. He and Stephanie are opening a travel agency after they're married. He told me tonight. So where would you like to go on your honeymoon? He owes me."

Kelcy reached up and pulled Hawk close to kiss him. "Oh, darling, I do love you," she whispered. "Was that a proposal?"

"Hmm, I believe it was, my love," he laughed. "What do you say?"

"Yes!" Kelcy beamed.

"In that case, let's not wait for Glen's agency to open. The company plane is at the airport. We'll elope tonight." Hawk scooped her up into his arms and smothered her with kisses. "You know, Kelcy, I've been thinking the lower part of the mill would make a great art gallery for you to operate. And you could display your own paintings, too. We'll talk about it."

"Talk," Kelcy answered. "Mmm, who wants to talk?" And she kissed him once more.